"**P**eter Archer is my name. I prefer Pete."

Pete pulled away his hand quickly and avoided making eye contact with Walter who was assessing him like he was a puppy he had found on the street. He chafed under Walter's regard. He barely stopped himself from fidgeting. This Walter fellow was so big and tall; he couldn't see around him.

He had depended on his senses to keep him alive so far, and now all his senses were telling him to run.

"I see, Pete it is then," Walter said. "Come this way. Matthew was going to take you to see Preston Wiley."

"The big boss?" Pete whispered fearfully.

"Yes, the big boss," Walter smiled, "and my big brother."

FOR PETE'S SAKE

BRENDA BARRETT

ALSO BY BRENDA BARRETT

FULL CIRCLE
NEW BEGINNINGS
THE PREACHER AND THE PROSTITUTE
AFTER THE END
THE EMPTY HAMMOCK
THE PULL OF FREEDOM
REBOUND SERIES
THREE RIVERS SERIES
NEW SONG SERIES
BANCROFT SERIES
MAGNOLIA SISTERS SERIES
SCARLETT SERIES
WILEY BROTHERS SERIES

ABOUT THE AUTHOR

Books have always been a big part of life for Jamaican born Brenda Barrett, she reports that she gets withdrawal symptoms if she does not consume at least two books per week. That is all she can manage these days, as her days are filled with writing, a natural progression from her love of reading. Currently, Brenda has several novels on the market, she writes predominantly in the historical fiction, Christian fiction, comedy and romance genres.

Apart from writing fictional books, Brenda writes for her blogs blackhair101.com; where she gives hair care tips and fiwibooks.com, where she shares about her writing life.

You can connect with Brenda online at:
Brenda-Barrett.com
Twitter.com/AuthorWriterBB
Facebook.com/AuthorBrendaBarrett

Chapter One

"**M**r. Preston Wiley, thank you so much for this interview. Your secretary said that she wasn't sure that you had the time." Denise gazed at her handsome interviewee and tried not to drool.

Preston nodded and looked at his watch. "I am pressed for time today. Is ten minutes okay? What was your name again?"

"Denise Graham, from Caribbean Finance Magazine. I am not sure that ten minutes will do, sir. Your life is a fascinating one. We covered you before in our Millionaires Under Twenty-five issue, and we got hints of a great story. We thought that this time around we would feature you on the cover and run your life story."

"My life story?" Preston furrowed his brow and then chuckled. "I am not too keen on my life story being in the public sphere, Denise."

A knock on the door interrupted their conversation, and a

striking looking man walked into the office.

"Sorry to interrupt." His voice sounded less than apologetic, but Denise was not paying that any mind. She was too awestruck even to process the thought. He had a faint resemblance to Preston Wiley, so she concluded that he was one of the Wiley brothers, he had to be. This one was certifiably hot.

"Can I have a quick word with you Preston?"

"Hello there." He smiled at her warmly.

How do the females in this building get any work done? Denise thought dazedly.

"This is Denise from Caribbean Finance Magazine," Preston said to his brother, "and Denise this is Walter Wiley, vice president of Finance."

"Nice to meet you." Denise nodded at Walter. "Is it possible for me to get a mini-interview with you too Walter?"

"Oh, not today." Walter glanced at his watch. "Call my assistant and set it up though. I think I can accommodate you later this week."

"Thank you." Denise nodded.

Preston got up and they headed to the far corner of the office where they stood shoulder-to-shoulder and whispered about God knows what.

Denise wished she could hear, but she would settle for observing them. What an eyeful it was.

She was a professional journalist who had been covering people in business for well nigh two decades, but it did not take a genius to figure out that the Wiley brothers were a fascinating bunch.

Goodness, if everything she had heard about Preston Wiley and his brothers was true, she had an epic article on her hands.

So far the accounts of how handsome they were held true.

Maybe everything else was as well. She had a whole bunch of notes from reliable sources about their fascinating lives.

There were stories about how they grew up without parents. How one set of them, she wasn't sure which set, had a mother who killed the other mother because she got tired of sharing her husband, Joseph Wiley.

If their father looked anything like them, I can understand why women were willing to share him and kill for him, Denise thought morbidly.

The brothers had hooded eyes, short straight noses, pronounced cheekbones and full lips and they were both tall, maybe over six feet.

Standing beside each other now the differences between the two brothers were obvious. Preston was leanly muscular. He looked more like he had a swimmers body. His hair was clipped close to his head, and he was cleanly shaven.

Walter, on the other hand, was muscular and thick. She could see through his dress shirt that he had some serious biceps especially standing as he was now with his arms folded. He had a neat mustache and beard combo going on that made him look even more attractive.

When two sets of brown eyes suddenly turned her way she resisted the urge to pretend that she hadn't been observing them intently.

They had caught her looking. The only thing she could do was withstand the stares, not breaking eye contact until Walter told them goodbye and strode away from the office.

"Walter just brought a matter to my attention…can we walk and talk? I have to go deal with this situation," Preston said when he came back over to the desk.

"Sure." Denise jumped up, "It would be nice to see you in action."

Preston frowned. "Unfortunately, you won't be seeing

me in action. What I am about to do, does not require my area of expertise as the company president; I rarely handle situations like this."

"What is it?" Denise was intrigued.

Preston opened the office door for her. "After you."

"Thank you." Denise smiled.

"A young man just attempted to steal some goods. He is at the Security Center. I hope you wore comfortable shoes," Preston said as they headed down the hallway and towards the elevator of the central administration building.

"I did." Denise looked down at her red pumps. She had come prepared for a tour of the head office of Wiley Corp.

It was a relatively large complex. A Wiley Groceries supermarket, the core business, was at the heart of the place and the various other companies which were Wiley run, were arranged in a neat U fanning out beside the supermarket. They also had a huge parking lot that was almost always full, even in the nights. She knew because she was a regular shopper.

There was the farming supplies store that was run by Guy Wiley, an architect's firm that was run by Jordan Wiley and a recording studio where Case Wiley, the famous gospel singer, and producer, spent most of his time.

This was indeed the Wiley brothers' headquarters. Her editor had requested a feature with all the brothers. Denise was almost salivating at the thought. It was hard to get them all in one place, so she was fortunate to get Preston Wiley, the head of the company.

She had also interviewed Jordan Wiley, a few years ago for the millionaires under twenty-five and she had wanted both him and Preston to do a joint feature, but it was not meant to be. Jordan was in Dubai finishing up a building project.

Architecture was his passion. She remembered how

excited he was about the subject when she spoke to him over the phone.

She dragged her mind from Jordan Wiley and focused on the current Wiley.

What was so special about a young man that stole goods? This was Kingston, even though they had state of the art security, they must catch shoplifters on a regular basis and dealt with them accordingly.

"Can we get on with the interview?" Preston asked when they got on the elevator. "As I said, today is not exactly ideal in terms of time."

"Oh yes, sorry." Denise whipped out her recorder and turned it on.

"Mr. Wiley, can you tell me about your beginnings, where were you born, that sort of thing?"

"Call me Preston." He looked at the recorder and then at her and shook his head, "Necessary evil, huh?"

She nodded. "I transcribe my notes from it.."

"Okay," Preston shrugged, "I was born in Portland, Jamaica. Have you been there?"

"Me?" Denise smiled, "just once…a wedding at a gorgeous hotel there. I thought how unspoiled it seemed…a place with potential."

"It's a very nice place," Preston said, "very rustic. I try to go back every month or so."

"And your parents," Denise asked, "are they still alive?"

They exited the elevator, and Preston glanced at her.

"It is common knowledge that my mother killed my father, his mistress and his mistress' sister and then herself, leaving six boys and three baby girls behind. She did it on my thirteenth birthday. Needless to say, my birthdays tend not to be very happy ones. That kind of event has a tendency to follow you around."

"Wow! So how did all of you manage?"

"Ah well, the Pryce girls were taken by their brother and his wife. And the six boys were left in the care of my mother's cousin, Fred and the housekeeper Pamela Stone. Fred was appointed our official guardian. At the time, he was heading up the supermarket business and living at the house. I guess it was the practical solution to not have us move and to keep the boys together. My brother Jordan was having none of it though. He would not leave our father's house."

"How old was he?" Denise asked.

"Twelve." Preston smiled. "He lived alone from the age of twelve."

"And what about the rest of you?" Denise asked as they headed across the lobby to the main entrance of the building.

"We were good for a while," Preston said wryly, "but then we found out that Fred was a gambler and he was not very careful with our inheritance. He wrecked the business by the time Jordan and I turned sixteen. We lost everything, the house, the businesses..."

"Oh, wow!" Denise looked at the large complex. "So how did you come from zero to this in twelve years?"

"It wasn't easy," Preston said. They headed toward the building that said Wiley Security Services.

"Fortunately for us, our father had the foresight to have an investment at the bank that was quite substantial. He saved all thirteen years of profit distribution from running Wiley Groceries. It matured that summer when we thought we had nothing left."

"Amazing, what a coincidence." Denise breathed.

"I don't believe in coincidences." Preston smiled. "I firmly believe that God knows the beginning from the end and he makes provisions for unforeseen circumstances."

"Amen," Denise murmured. "So what did you do with

your windfall?"

"The four oldest boys went to college. I went to the local college on a scholarship; Jordan went to the University of the West Indies open campus in Portland. We both did business studies.

"As soon as we hit eighteen we bought back the businesses from the bank and worked like crazy to get them back in black. Those early years were crazy-no-sleep years. We had one goal, and that was to become profitable again while we juggled school.

"All the brothers had to work. It was not an option. Unfortunately, we didn't have the luxury of being typical teenagers. There was no time for anything else in our life."

"Oh, come on." Denise looked impressed. "You never had a girlfriend?"

"I had no time for relationships," Preston said shaking his head. "Between helping our youngest brothers, running a household and two supermarkets I only started looking around when I was twenty-two. I had a semi-serious relationship when I was twenty-three."

"Have you forgotten how to have fun?" Denise asked smiling, "all work and no play..."

"These days I play," Preston said glancing at Denise. "I understand the need for play and also for balance. Now that we have a Wiley Groceries in every parish in Jamaica and we have competent managers and staff. I can breathe a little."

"And how do you relax?" Denise asked they were standing in the middle of the foyer of Wiley Securities.

"I go to Portland. I have a villa there. I snorkel, fish, play tennis and read. My brother Guy is always recommending books to me."

"It sounds tame for a young man of twenty-seven." Denise raised an eyebrow skeptically.

"It is the pace I like." Preston grinned. "Slow, is a welcome pace compared to the catastrophe of my growing up years."

"Any of the Wiley brothers married yet?" Denise asked eagerly, too eagerly.

"No." Preston chuckled at her expression, "but my brother Saint is engaged. He will get married in May."

"And you? When are you planning to tie the knot?" Denise asked.

"I don't know," Preston answered the questioned contemplatively. "I have never really thought about it. I like to think I have plenty of time."

"Have you broken any hearts?" Denise asked.

"This is on the record?" Preston eyed the recorder and then laughed. "I am not sure if I have. None of my relationships have been long term. As I said, I have been obscenely busy through the years."

"Any regrets in your life so far?" Denise asked smiling.

She was surprised that Preston took a long time to respond. So long in fact that she thought he wasn't going to bother answering.

When he did, he did so with surprising honesty. "Yes, I have one regret. I wouldn't call it a regret more like a mistake I made. Sometimes, I find myself dwelling on it, and I wonder about it especially now that I have more downtime."

"Is it business or personal?" Denise asked.

"Personal, very personal," Preston said, and then he looked across the lobby as a tall, fit gentleman in gym gear strode towards them.

He had the high forehead and the hooded eyes of the Wiley's, but surely he couldn't be a Wiley. He had green eyes, and he was light skinned.

Denise stared in fascination as he came towards them.

"I have him in the holding room," The guy said to Preston.

"Let me know how it goes. Call me. I am late for an appointment."

He strode away with Denise looking after him in puzzlement.

"Who is he?"

"That is my brother, Saint. He heads Wiley Security."

"Oh my goodness, he is fine." Denise breathed.

Preston laughed out loud, "That is the reaction that Saint usually gets when he steps into a room. He and Case are the designated heartthrobs of the Wiley brothers."

"You would all get that reaction. I can't imagine the six of you together in the same room. The ladies wouldn't know where to look."

Preston laughed. "Thank you for the compliment, Denise, but I am afraid that this is where I have to leave you. I have to deal with this shoplifting situation privately."

"What is so special about this person?" Denise asked curiously.

"Turn off the recorder first," Preston said waiting for her to turn it off.

She did quickly.

"Well this young man, claims to be the grandson of our former housekeeper Pamela Stone, the one who took care of us after our parents died. I am just going to verify. If he is her grandson, then you must understand that this is a special situation."

"Yes, yes, maybe that could be something for another article?" Denise nodded vigorously. "As it is now, I have more than enough information for my current article. Thank you for your time, Preston. "

Preston nodded. "I hope it will be a good one, and that Wiley Incorporated will be highlighted favorably."

"Yes, definitely." Denise nodded.

She watched in admiration as he headed toward the holding area. His mind was already a million miles away from the magazine article.

Chapter Two

Preston looked through the glass of the holding area at the boy who claimed he was Pamela Stone's grandson.

The boy was dirty, to put it mildly. His hair was matted and looked like a bird's nest. His face was so obscured with dirt Preston couldn't see his features. He was slim and lanky.

He had tears streaming down his face; they left behind dirty track lines, which disappeared under his chin.

"What did he say his name was?" Preston asked Matthew, Saint's assistant, who was standing beside him and shaking his head in pity.

"He said his name was Pete Archer and that he came to Kingston to find his grandmother Pamela Stone. He won't give us any information after that. He just started crying, said he was hungry that's why he tried to take a bun and a drink from the supermarket.

"When Saint heard the name Pamela Stone, he called Walter…Walter called you."

"Have you fed him?" Preston asked, looking at the little boy again.

"Yes, sir. Walter gave him his lunch. He ate that and then he ate mine."

"Goodness, he was probably starving." Preston leaned closer to the glass. "He needs a bath and a trim. Arrange that and then bring him to my office."

"Yes, sir." Matthew nodded. "Shouldn't we call the child development agency?"

"Not yet," Preston said. "I'll handle it."

He headed back to his office, his mind whirling with thoughts about who this little boy could be and what it all meant. He had not heard from Miss Pam in twelve years. He had no idea how she or Sheryl had fared.

Sadly, he had been so taken up with his own life and that of his brothers that he had not had the time to think about them apart from the passing echoes of guilt that usually hit around his birthday.

Miss Pam and Sheryl had joined the list of things to be sorry about on that particular day.

It was fairly recently that Jordan had brought them up in conversation. They had been reminiscing and talking about Fred.

Poor unfortunate Fred whose body the coastal guards had found washed up on the shores in Cayman, ten years ago. The police had speculated that he was murdered. They were still not sure. Maybe Fred had messed with the wrong people because of his gambling addiction.

After they talked about Fred, they had started talking about Sheryl and that forbidden night and then it had hit him afresh how irresponsible he had been.

He had enjoyed himself at the expense of a mentally ill girl. He wondered now if Sheryl had gotten help if she had the baby.

Obviously, she had a baby if the little boy in his security-holding cell was to be believed and if he was right about Pamela Stone, their former housekeeper, being his grandmother.

Miss Pam had only one child, and that was Sheryl, but Miss Pam had also been a stickler for discipline and decency. How could her grandson be in this state?

And what on earth happened to Sheryl for a child of hers to look like this?

Miss Pam had not pursued the statutory rape case against the fake doctor, Sam Fay.

He had disappeared from the area shortly after that because people had begun to realize that he was a quack and had started demanding refunds for the fake medication they had gotten from him.

Miss Pam had left soon after that episode as well. Preston did not get the chance to say a proper goodbye. She had left them a handwritten note telling them to be good boys and then she had exited the house as if she had not lived there. Most of the boys had left by that time to go to live at their father's house anyway.

Miss Pam's job had been redundant. She had no children to care for and an almost empty house to maintain.

He had felt bad about not telling her the truth about him and Sheryl, but he couldn't have told her without it causing even more upheaval in their lives.

That was his main regret. He should have been responsible enough to tell her. It had not only been a rough time for him; it probably had been a horrible time for her as well. She was out of a job and had a mentally ill and pregnant daughter to care for.

Had they recovered from that episode? What if they hadn't?

Preston thought as he entered the elevator.

What if they had moved back to Kingston and were living in abject poverty? Surely they would have contacted him? Wiley Incorporated was mentioned often enough in business magazines and local financial programs.

At least Miss Pam could contact one of them if she was in dire straits. And what had become of Sheryl? Was she wandering the streets eating from garbage bins or had Miss Pam wised up and gotten her checked over by a real doctor?

He needed to know these things.

He was now feverishly running through in his mind all the mentally ill females he had seen on the streets. He couldn't remember their faces. Could one of them have been Sheryl?

Goodness.

The need to know was urgent; it was gnawing at him like an untended itch.

He headed straight to his secretary's spacious office. Helena was on the phone when he got there. He waited until she finished the call.

To him, Helena was the best assistant on the face of the planet. She was very efficient. She anticipated his needs sometimes before he even thought of it and best of all, she knew everybody. She picked up more news than a news outlet and had more contacts than the yellow pages.

"That was Arnold White's secretary," Helena said. "He wanted to know if you were coming to his annual charity gala next weekend. It will be in Portland at his private villa. Black tie, a couple thousand dollars per plate."

"Ask Walter to go," Preston said. "I am all partied out and the year has not even started properly. Walter won't mind another party, that's his thing."

"Okay." Helena jotted that down. "How may I help you? You look troubled."

"Yes, I am troubled." Preston sat across from her and sighed. "I have a little problem. At the security center is a scruffy little boy who looks like he has been living on the streets. He claims he is the grandson of my former housekeeper, Pamela Stone.

"I need to find her and her daughter, Sheryl Stone. A detailed update about the two of them would be welcomed."

"Got you." Helena nodded. "When do you want this?"

"Is today possible?" He raised an eyebrow. "Can you wave around your magician wand and make it happen?"

"Nah." Helena shook her head. "I know a guy, but he is not that fast. However, if you give me more details, I can do some sniffing of my own on social media. Who needs a detective these days? People want you to find them."

"I only have a few details. Twelve years ago Miss Pam was a housekeeper at our place in Portland. She liked to cook and bake, and she forced us to eat our vegetables, and she was a stickler for manners, and she used to listen to me talk on and on while she made jam or fruit cake or whatever it is she was making." Preston shrugged. "Just the very thought of those first couple of months makes me feel warm inside."

Helena tucked her hand under her chin and smiled. "She was good to you?"

"Very." Preston nodded. "I don't know if any of that information would help. I have no idea of her address or anything like that; all I know is that she came back to Kingston with Sheryl in 2000."

"No," Helena shook her head, "she is an older person, probably not very social media savvy. Tell me about her daughter. How old was she?"

"Fifteen." Preston cleared his throat. "She was stunning."

Helena chuckled. "She was, was she?"

"Yep, she had the prettiest mahogany eyes with a darker

brown around them, and she had smooth honey brown skin and the pinkest lips."

"My boss had a crush." Helena chuckled. "Or should I say has. It sounds like you are still smitten."

"No." Preston refocused on Helena. "How could I be? I have no idea how Sheryl is these days. People change. Circumstances change. I need to know how much has changed for them so that I can make it right if I need to. I owe them."

"What school or church did she attend while in Kingston?" Helena asked, "that is a good place to start."

"She attended the Queens School for girls. She was in a grade higher than Jordan and me even though she was a year younger. Miss Pam was convinced that she was a genius."

"Ooh," Helena jotted that down, "that's decent info. I was a Queens School old girl, of course, I would have been a couple years before Sheryl, but we have an active past students association. I will see if she is registered with one of our chapters. It's possible, even though she spent only a year, once a queen always a queen."

"Yep, she was pretty proud of her school and hated that she was transferred. She sang in the choir, and she liked the colors blue and green but especially liked the two mixed together."

"Turquoise? Helena wrinkled her nose, "I don't think that is relevant."

"Her favorite dish was fried chicken and mashed potatoes, she made a little snort when she laughed, and she resented the fact that she had to wear glasses to read, she thought it made her look nerdish."

"Aww." Helena chuckled. "So what on earth separated you two? I mean you should have at least kept in touch with this adorable sounding girl."

"It's a long story." Preston shook his head and got up. "Send Matthew in with the boy when they call up from the lobby."

"Sure thing." Helena nodded. "When is her birthday?"

"September 7th," Preston said. "She was born at home."

"You sure do remember a lot of specifics about her," Helena muttered under her breath.

"I heard that." Preston headed to his office. "Just tell your investigator guy that this is urgent."

"Most definitely." Helena nodded. "**Virtue et sapientia floreat.**"

Preston paused and looked around, "What does that mean?"

"May she flourish in virtue and wisdom." Helena smiled, "our school motto and my wishes for Sheryl."

Preston nodded. "I hope she has flourished in virtue and wisdom."

He desperately hoped so, but he felt a foreboding so strong that he had to close his eyes and lean on the door. If Sheryl or Miss Pam had flourished why was that little dirty boy downstairs?

****

Preston was itching to call Jordan about this current situation. He hated that Jordan was so far away in Dubai, which was nine hours ahead of Jamaican time. He missed their lunches together every day and rehashing things out with him or just talking. This current situation would have given him a worry partner, somebody he could bounce questions off and share theories with.

Preston picked up his cell phone and glanced at the clock. Jordan would probably be in bed now. It was nine o'clock in the night Dubai time.

He dialed the number anyway, this couldn't wait, and

Jordan would be angry if he told him this kind of news long after the fact.

He waited for Jordan to pick up, swung his chair to the bank of windows behind him and looked out. They were located beside an empty lot with a football field, quite close to several upper-class neighborhoods.

Jordan was the one who had heard about their current location being on sale, and he had been the one who had designed the complex. He was a good architect, Preston had to admit. He had begged and implored Jordan through the years to stick to the supermarket business.

At first, he had wanted Jordan to lose interest in architecture and join him, but from the get-go, Jordan had been firm with what he wanted.

"I am just helping out," Jordan used to say after they had one of their power meetings. "I am not going to be here for much longer. I want to do my own thing. This is your thing. You were born for this."

Ironically, if it weren't for Jordan, he wouldn't have a supermarket to run. Jordan could have kept their father's investment a secret. He could have hoarded it or hidden it or spent it because his name was the only one on that account.

Instead, he had sat down with Preston and solemnly looked at him with the bank book opened in front of him.

"I hope you can make this work bro. I am giving it all to you to invest in getting us back on our feet. I am confident that you can do it. You will be better at this supermarket thing than your grandfather, and your father put together, and all of us will benefit from your efforts. Just remember we are all counting on you."

Ironically, Hannah's children were not into the core supermarket business. As soon as the business was stabilized and was doing well, they left to do what they wanted. Guy went into farming. He had a near twenty-acre strawberry farm in the foothills of the Blue Mountain. He also had the farm store, which was doing exceptionally well.

Case was a singer. They had entered him into a local gospel competition when he was thirteen, and he had won. He was signed to an international label now and was well known.

As for Jordan, five years ago he had gotten his masters in civil engineering and had left the supermarket business completely.

"Hello," Jordan's sleepy voice echoed in his ear. "What's up bro?"

Preston couldn't stop the pleased smile that spread across his face.

"When are you coming home?" Preston asked, "Lots of things are going on here that you need to know."

"I just spoke to you yesterday." Jordan cleared his throat noisily. "What on earth could happen between now and then? Is it Saint. He is still getting married, isn't he? No glitches with the wife to be?"

"No glitches." Preston leaned back in his chair. "It is still on for May 10. You had better be here two weeks before. Go again."

Jordan sighed. "I will be, I cannot miss the first Wiley marriage from the lot. So who else is something wrong with? It can't be Walter. He called me last week, and he sounded like all was well except for that church sister who was pursuing him aggressively."

Preston chuckled. "Ladies are always pursuing Walter aggressively. He is fine."

"It's not Guy; he is thrilled with his farm. He said he is ready for me to design and build his villa when I get back. Who knows when that will be?"

"Ah," Preston murmured, "you still threatening to stay in

Dubai, that's so far away from us. I actually understood being away for two years but, Jordy, you are killing me here."

"We were talking about the news that you wanted to share." Jordan was itching to change the subject.

Preston wasn't going to let him off so quickly; he still had no idea why Jordan had taken a Dubai job halfway around the world.

"I thought your wanderlust had been fulfilled. Your contract will soon be up. Please don't renew it."

"I don't know," Jordan said vaguely. "I am still weighing my options. Is the news about Case? It can't be. I spoke to him a couple of minutes ago. His US tour is going well; he sounds happy he is touring with some big names."

"Which leaves?" Preston prompted playfully.

"You." Jordan chuckled. "The very obvious first guess. What's wrong?"

"There is a boy downstairs who claims to be Miss Pam's grandson. They caught him trying to steal from the supermarket. He confessed that he was in Kingston trying to find his grandmother, Pamela Stone."

"Our Pamela Stone?" Jordan asked skeptically.

"Not sure yet," Preston murmured.

"How does he look? How old is he?" Jordan fired off the questions rapidly.

"He was so dirty, I couldn't tell." Preston rubbed his hand over his face. "He looks to be about ten/eleven. He is thin though, and I didn't see him get up, so I don't know if he is tall."

"Could he be...is he?" Jordan cleared his throat, "he could be your son if he is eleven. You know that right?"

"I know," Preston muttered. "Or maybe he is not even related to Miss Pam, and I am just paranoid. I haven't spoken to him yet."

"I don't care what time it is when you speak to him, call me," Jordan said, "and try to find out more about the whereabouts of Sheryl and Miss Pam."

"I've already put Helena on that." Preston sighed.

"If he is your son..." Jordan's voice trailed off, "it would be something wouldn't it?"

"It would be something," Preston said fear gripping his chest. "It would mean I had failed Sheryl twelve years ago and that I have a son who looks like he is living on the streets and robbing his own family's supermarket."

"Or it could mean that this is your second chance," Jordan said faintly the phone connection was fading. "You do right by him. Even if he is not yours."

"Yes," Preston murmured. "I plan to."

Chapter Three

Pete thought he was in deep trouble when the security caught him earlier. He had been hungry enough to pass out, or they wouldn't have run him down like they did and caught him. He could outrun most adults, and for the past four months, he had done just that.

Some people were not very nice, and some of them were too nice. Both sets of folks had tried to impede his trek to Kingston.

His journey to Kingston had involved lots of running and walking and begging. It had taken him six weeks to reach Kingston from Westmoreland. He had stopped in certain places when it had seemed interesting enough and when it had been beneficial to his journey, like the weekend church camp where he had got his new shoes. They were now tattered.

He had even spent a week on a farm in St. Catherine. He had helped to plant peanuts. He had slept in a hut with some of the other men; gotten three square meals a day… they hadn't asked him many questions.

When his week of helping out was over, he had continued with his journey. Nothing could dissuade him from coming to Kingston and fulfilling his mission.

He had been feeling quite proud of himself for making it this far and surviving on his own. But his luck had run out.

Because today he had felt the sharp agonizing pain of hunger, unlike any pain he had encountered before. It had gnawed at him, scrambled his insides, and made him feel as if he would just expire where he stood.

He knew better than to steal. Before Miss Constance left them at the boys home, she had taught him right from wrong.

Lying and stealing were at the very top of the worst sins to ever commit. She had them recite the Ten Commandments and the ones about bearing false witness and stealing she would sit them down and talk about for hours.

He expected the wrath of God to rain down on him right about now. He wasn't sure whose punishment he would welcome most now, God's or the supermarket security. He would be locked up for sure.

The tall, stern security man came back to the place where they were holding him and took him to what looked like an office and through to a bathroom. Two ladies in blue uniforms were waiting for him.

They had on masks and gloves, one of them had cutting shear in her hand. Were they going to hurt him before they sent him to prison?

"What's your name?" One of the lady's asked through her mask.

"Pete…Peter," he stuttered.

"You are going to bathe in there," The lady pointed to a bathroom, "and then we are going to cut your hair. Clean underwear and clothes are hanging by the door. Leave your dirty stuff in the passageway."

Pete walked tentatively toward where they pointed. He had not had a bath in close to a month, at least not a good wash, bathing in the rain and having his clothes dry on him did not count. They probably had on the masks because of him.

The bathroom was more beautiful than any that he had ever been in. It was large and spacious and had an array of soaps still in their wrapper on the ledge. There was a large body wash with a rag sitting at the side of the tub. He figured that was his to use. It lay near a clean set of jeans and a white t-shirt.

He hurriedly undressed leaving his clothes in the passageway. He purposefully avoided the mirror and got into the bath. The warm water was sublime. He scrubbed himself for more than five times, and he spent a long time in the shower. One of the women knocked on the door to check up on him countless times.

He didn't know when he would get this kind of bath again and he was savoring it. He knew what would happen; next, they would call the police who would call the children authorities and then he would be placed back into a boys home, or worse a juvenile facility.

The boys home in Westmoreland probably reported him missing already. He had climbed out through a window in the dead of night and run like he was in danger, though he wasn't.

They had been perfectly nice people, but he was not used to group living and the institutionalized air of the home. He had wanted to go back to his foster mother Miss Constance, but Miss Constance was not there anymore.

After nearly forty years of fostering children, she had retired. She had locked up her house and moved to another area to be closer to her biological children. She had given him and three others back to the state. She was tired she had told him, tired of dealing with other people's children when hers needed the help.

He had lived with her for five years after his adopted parents had died in a car accident. Her place was what he remembered of being a home.

He scrubbed his hair thoroughly with the body wash, but it wasn't helping matters it was matted and stiff feeling.

When he finally came out of the shower, the bathroom was cloudy with steam, but at least he was clean. He wiped off the mirror and looked at himself. Maybe they would have some mercy on him and not send him to a juvenile facility he would hate that more than boys home.

He hurriedly put on the clean clothes and the shoes and socks. They had taken away the dirty ones. He looked down at his feet—he had not worn socks for a long time. His last pair had been threadbare; the tips of them had completely disintegrated.

"Feeling better now?" The lady asked him when he went back into the office. "The clothes fit?"

"Yes...er...very much." He answered politely. "The clothes fit very well thanks."

She indicated to a swivel chair for him to sit and then put a cape around his neck.

"Ahm, what are they going to do to me?" He asked when they started to shear his hair. It fell down his neck in matted balls of curls.

"I have no clue," The lady murmured, "the bosses' boss wanted us to make you presentable for the bigger boss."

"The bigger boss?" Pete's mouth ran dry. "Then what is he going to do to me?"

"I have no clue," the lady said again. "All done."

She brushed him off and removed the cape.

The other gentleman from earlier came into the room and stood looking at him for a while, squinting his eyes and assessing him.

"I'll be damned." He finally chuckled. "This is something."

"What?" Pete finally croaked out the question.

The ladies stood beside the man and were nodding as they looked at him as well.

"He's a sweet looking boy without the dirt and matted hair," the lady who trimmed him said fondly. "He's going to grow up to be a real looker…Like the big boss."

"Exactly like the big boss. This is quite a coincidence," the man said and then indicated to him. "Come on."

"Where are we going?" Pete's lips trembled. "Please, can I just go? I promise that I won't steal anything again. I was just so hungry."

"Where would you go?" The man asked, escorting him from the office.

"I want to find Pamela Stone," Pete said. "That's all."

"And what if you don't find her?" The man asked. "You will be hungry again and steal again."

Pete considered his statement and sighed. It was true.

"Besides, there must be people looking for you. How old are you anyway?"

"Eleven," Pete said grumpily. "People might have been looking for me, but I am sure they probably gave up by now."

"Your parents would not give up looking for you." The man snorted. "They must be worried sick."

"I don't have parents," Pete said. "I was in foster care, and then my foster mother decided that she did not want to bother with other people's kids, so she sent us back into the system."

"Oh," the guy looked at him sympathetically. "How long

have you been on the streets?"

"Four months," Pete whispered. "I came all the way from Westmoreland to find Pamela Stone."

"Westmoreland?" The man exclaimed. "Are you serious, that's more than a hundred miles."

"I walked most of it. Took me six weeks," Pete said proudly.

"How did you eat, where did you sleep?"

They stepped into an elevator in another building. Pete looked around; everything seemed so impressive. The man was trying to distract him with his questions. He was going to be in real trouble very soon.

"I slept at churches; there is one every couple of steps. I chose the ones with a veranda. It was comfortable enough. I had my knapsack as a pillow. I ate at restaurants; the owners are very kind to starving children. All I did was tell them I was hungry. Nobody turned me away until I came to Kingston. People here are not as nice as in the country. I guess there are too many beggars around, people get annoyed."

"That's very perceptive, you speak and act older than any eleven-year-old I have spoken with." The man looked at him appreciatively. "What made you choose to steal from this supermarket?"

"I didn't exactly steal anything, you guys caught me before I could," Pete said defensively. "I chose this place because it looked so pretty with a lot of fancy vehicles in the parking lot and I was feeling faint. I thought I would find a sympathetic person to tell that I was hungry but when I stepped into the supermarket, nobody paid me any attention, they started going in the other direction."

The elevator door opened and they stepped into a carpeted hallway. It smelled clean and fresh, kind of like Miss Constance's Ocean Breeze fabric softener that she liked to put on the bed linen.

He wanted to stop for a while and savor the smell.

The man led him down a corridor past several offices with glass enclosures. He could not get to read the names on the doors.

One door was opened when they passed. Matthew slowed down and waved to the man inside who was on the phone.

Pete read the name on the door, Walter Wiley, Vice President, Finance. The man in there hung up the phone and widened his eyes.

"Matthew, who do we have here?"

"The boy from downstairs. The one who ate your lunch."

"Oh my goodness." The man he assumed was Walter exclaimed. "Let me take this from here."

"Okay, I understand." Matthew looked at Pete and held out his hand. "This is where we part, buddy. All the best."

Pete shook his hand feeling suddenly bereft.

This guy Matthew had been familiar to Pete for a little while now, but he was in uncharted waters now with this new man who was acting pretty strange. The man subjected him to a long perusal and then held out his hand for a shake.

"My name is Walter Wiley. What is your name?"

Pete looked at his outstretched hand suspiciously and then finally took it when the man didn't withdraw his.

"Peter Archer is my name. I prefer Pete."

Pete pulled away his hand quickly and avoided making eye contact with Walter who was assessing him like he was a puppy he had found on the street. He chafed under Walter's regard. He barely stopped himself from fidgeting. This Walter fellow was so big and tall; he couldn't see around him.

He had depended on his senses to keep him alive so far, and now all his senses were telling him to run.

"I see, Pete it is then," Walter said. "Come this way.

Matthew was going to take you to see Preston Wiley."

"The big boss?" Pete whispered fearfully.

"Yes, the big boss," Walter smiled, "and my big brother."

Pete imagined a man who was even more humongous than this Walter giant, and he shuddered inside. Genuine fear had him in its clutches.

They passed more offices, or at least he assumed they were offices. They had names on the doors, a lot of vice presidents for various things.

And then they came to the end of the building. It had an alcove that looked like a mini library. There were glass shelves everywhere that were decorated with various objects where he imagined books would be. One of them was a large clear bowl that was filled with colorful candy. He wondered if the candy was real.

A lady was sitting behind a glass desk. She was on the phone, and she smiled when she saw them coming. She looked a lot like Regina, the principal from the Steve Harvey Show except that her hair was dyed blonde.

"Walter," she said hanging up the phone.

Pete was distracted by the phone. It was all clear; he could see the wires in the thing.

"Helena," Walter said, "I need to see Preston, he is free, isn't he?

"He is now. Wait a minute." Helena held up a finger. "Is this the boy from downstairs?"

"Yes." Walter nodded.

"I thought Matthew was taking him up." Helena subjected him to the same scrutiny that Walter had earlier. He was beginning to feel self-conscious, what was up with these people and their long stares?

"Now I understand the interest in him," Helena finally said. "He is a dead ringer for Preston."

Pete shuddered. *Dead ringer what was that?* Were they going to kill him?

He looked down the hallway frightfully. He should make a run for it. He was feeling stronger now, and the shoes were more comfortable. It was a straight line down to the bank of elevators, but after that, he had no idea what to do. Today was his first trip in an elevator.

And then he felt Walter's hand on his shoulders trapping him, holding him in one place.

"What's a dead ringer?" He asked fearfully. "Are you people going to kill me?"

"A dead ringer is when you look like someone else," Walter said gently. "And no, we are not going to kill you, far from it. The Wiley brothers do not kill their own."

He opened the door to the big boss' office with his hand still on his shoulders.

"Surprise, it's a boy," Walter said to the man who was sitting at the desk.

Chapter Four

I have a son, Preston thought faintly. The boy was pure Wiley. He would do a DNA test of course, but he knew a carbon copy when he saw one. And this was one.

He glanced at Walter who pushed the boy further into the room and then sat down.

"Where should we begin?" Walter asked raising an eyebrow.

"Introductions would be nice." Preston ignored Walter and his obvious hankering for information and instead focused on the child.

He held out his hand to the boy who looked at it fearfully.

"My name is Preston Wiley." Preston inhaled raggedly, trying to get his bearings after such an unexpected surprise. Looking at the boy was like looking at a past picture. It was pretty disconcerting.

"I knew Pamela Stone, very well," he continued. "She used to take care of me when I was about the same age as you are right now."

"You knew her?" All the fear fled from the boy's face, and he seemed to relax a little, he took Preston's hands and vigorously shook it.

His hand felt thin and bony. Was he ever this small? Preston thought, as he sat back in his chair and looked at the boy.

"What is your name?"

"Peter Archer but everybody calls me Pete." His voice was confident and stronger. "I am trying to find Pamela Stone, do you know where she is?"

"I have no clue. We lost touch years ago, but I will find her," Preston said drinking in his little pointy face. Could this little miniature version of him see the resemblance between them?

Walter cleared his throat. "I am desperate to hear the story here, but I have to run. I am coming over to your place tonight."

Preston looked at his brother and nodded. "Yes, sure."

When Walter left the office. Pete looked around while Preston observed him. He did not have any physical characteristics for his mom.

Nothing.

He even had the Wiley mole. A big black dot a little under his right ear. Goodness. His dad had it. All his brothers had it.

"What were you doing on the street?" Preston asked gently. "Where are you coming from and how on earth did you end up here?"

Pete looked at Preston and then sighed. "If I tell you how I ended up here will you take me back to the boys home?"

Preston gasped. "Boys home?"

Pete nodded. "Yes, I ran away from the one in Sav."

"That's at the other end of the island!" Preston struggled to keep his mouth shut; his mind was whirring with a hundred and one questions. "I will have to tell them where you are of course but I am not sending you back to a boys home. I will have my lawyers sort that out."

"Or prison?" Pete asked quickly. "I didn't steal your stuff."

"Or prison," Preston said wondering how he would break it to this kid that he was family, not just family, his own flesh and blood. The thought was taking a while to sink in. Pete would not be going to any prison, not on his watch.

"Tell me your story. Start from the beginning," Preston said after a pause. He watched while Pete having stated his demands, stopped looking at him and then at the ground.

"I was adopted by Daniel and Rita Archer when I was a baby. They died in a car accident when I was six." Pete kept looking at the ground.

"Daniel and Rita Archer." Preston leaned forward in his chair. "The names don't ring a bell."

"We lived at a place called Brompton. We had lots of mangoes trees…of every type." Pete finally found the courage to look up at Preston.

He was not as big and hulky looking as Walter Wiley. He may be the bigger brother but not in size. And he was kind.

Pete felt more relaxed. He could even look him in the face while he talked and not somewhere near his shirt collar.

There was something about Preston Wiley that felt familiar. He felt as if he could trust him. He didn't often feel that way about people when he just met them.

He leaned back in the chair; he had been perilously perched at the edge, ready for flight.

"So what did Daniel and Rita Archer do for work?" Preston asked giving him a reassuring smile.

That was enough to loosen Pete's tongue and make him even more relaxed. "My mom was a teacher at an infant school, and my dad managed a hotel in Black River. My foster mother, Miss Constance, said that the Archers' didn't have any family that was willing to take me in after they died because I wasn't a true blood relative."

"Ah," Preston nodded, "so that's where Miss Constance comes in?"

"Yes," Pete nodded, "I was sent to a foster home that was run by Miss Constance. I was there for five years. Earlier this year she decided that she was not going to do any more fostering, so I was sent to the boys home in Sav. I hate it there."

Preston winced. He had a son who was shuffled from one place to another like goods in a warehouse.

He felt a wave of guilt so overpowering he could barely speak.

"So, how do you know about Miss Pam?" He asked his voice barely a whisper as he grappled with the fact that he had partially caused this upheaval in Pete's life. Maybe Pete would have had a better time of it with him and his brothers in Portland.

"Her name was on the back of my adoption certificate, written in pencil," Pete answered his question. "It said Pamela Stone, grandmother, Kingston. I saw it when they were packing up my parent's stuff before they sent me into foster care."

"And you remember this from you were six?" Preston asked incredulously. "Wow."

"I kind of memorized it." Pete sighed, "I thought one day when I was older I would find Pamela Stone, my grandmother from Kingston. My blood family."

Pete's voice cracked up, and he looked away from Preston. "All I want is to belong to a family again. I hate the boys home. I pray about it every night. You know, I ask God to let me find Pamela Stone because she is my only real family and I..." Pete swallowed. "I can't go back to the boys home."

"Goodness," Preston muttered, he got up and went around the desk. "Come here."

Pete looked at him; big pools of unshed tears at the corner of his eyes. "Are you going to let me leave now so that I can find her?"

"No." Preston shook his head. "I want you to see something."

He walked over to the floor to ceiling mirror near the mini-conference table and beckoned for Pete to come with him.

Pete came reluctantly. He stooped down to Pete's level until they were the same height.

"What do you see?" Preston asked as Pete looked at their reflection.

"We have the same nose," Pete whispered.

"And forehead and eyes." Preston sighed. "You look a lot like me. Almost a carbon copy. It's amazing, isn't it?"

"Yes!" Pete nodded. "Why?"

"Because I know your mom." Preston sighed, "we were friends a couple of years before you were born, and we lived in the same house. And what I am trying to say is this," Preston looked at Pete, brown eyes to brown eyes connecting, "I am your father. I am your blood relative."

Pete gawped like he was gasping for air.

"I am your real family," Preston said slowly. The thought of it was still making him dizzy. "Which means you'll never be alone again. What's more, you have five uncles, Walter who just brought you in here and four others who will want to meet you very soon."

"Are you serious?" Pete whispered. "You are my father? But you are the big boss."

Preston chuckled. "Yes, that's right. Today you chose the

right supermarket to stop by. That prayer of yours worked, just not the way that you thought it would."

Pete threw his hand around Preston's neck and wouldn't let go for a long time.

****

"So he is really yours?" Walter asked incredulously. "How did this happen?"

"The usual way," Preston growled. "Keep your voice down he is sleeping upstairs. He was out like a light the minute I took him home."

"But you...I can't believe you." Walter got up and started pacing around the open plan living room. "You remember when I had the...uh...issue with Gia? You were on my case about my life and my choices, and having sex without commitment. Your lecture still gives me nightmares. You were worst than Pastor Tate."

"You were about to be kicked out of university for your relationship with Madam Gia, who took great pleasure in letting it be known that you were totally under her spell. I didn't want you to lose your scholarship or your place at university for that. That sex tape was terrible. All two minutes of it."

"It wasn't a sex tape." Walter hissed.

"You were dressed up in leather pants, her panties over your head and she was beating you with a whip. Just thinking about it makes me sick." Preston visibly shuddered.

"I was young, stupid unconverted…did I say stupid? We were role-playing." Walter said sheepishly. "She read some book about it and wanted to dominate me or something. I accommodated her little fantasy. She taped it."

"I say good riddance to Gia." Preston grimaced. "She

was bad news all around. I hope you are still not into that sort of thing. Her poor family was so embarrassed when the university administrator had us watch the tape. It was cringe city I'll tell you that."

Walter stopped pacing. "I was never into bondage and stuff like that, and yes it was cringe-worthy. Gia had a powerful effect on me."

"Like when she had you sneaking out to nightclubs and street dances in some dangerous areas." Preston frowned, "We worried about you."

"And I am grateful." Walter shook his head. "How did we start talking about my mistakes? We were talking about your obvious mistake, the one sleeping upstairs. I remember Sheryl; she was sex-crazed."

"Because of her head injury." Preston pointed out, "It messed with her brain."

"And you slept with a brain-injured girl?" Walter widened his eyes. "When? Miss Pam was like a police concerning Sheryl. That day when Sheryl accused one of the Wiley brothers of getting her pregnant I had thought it was a bad joke. I had never in a million years imagined that it could have been possible. Though for one minute when you were silent we got a little nervous."

"Well, it was possible. One night she came into my room and slid under the covers naked. I was a teenage boy running on hormones. I have no excuse." Preston sighed and ran his hand down his face.

"Does Jordan know?" Walter asked and then snorted, "but of course he does, you do nothing without discussing it with Jordan. You two are as thick as thieves. Did he sleep with her as well? If he did, I wouldn't be so sure that Pete is yours, you guys look so much alike."

"No, he didn't sleep with her." Preston shook his head.

"Just me. And I did not discuss the situation with Jordan. It was not something I planned."

"What are we going to do with him?" Walter asked heading for the fridge.

Preston smiled. He did not miss that 'we'.

The doorbell rang once, and he got up. He knew that would be either Saint or Guy.

"Hold that thought," he said to Walter. "I have a feeling I am going to have to repeat all of this."

Walter took out his leftover dinner and sniffed the container. "Yes, I understand, Can I get this?"

"Sure." Preston nodded, "That's a lot of food though."

Walter grunted.

Preston opened the door. Guy and Saint were standing in the doorway.

"News travels fast," Preston murmured.

He opened the door wider.

Saint walked in first and then Guy with a big hamper of strawberries. "I have goodies for the new nephew."

"You mean old nephew," Saint grunted, "Who was a street kid. He had five uncles and a father who could easily provide for him and yet when I saw him today he looked like something the cat dragged in. Explain to me how he got this way."

Saint turned pale green eyes on Preston, and he sighed. "Maybe I should call Jordan and Case, and we do this at once."

"Cool," Guy said cheerily as he placed the big basket of strawberries on the counter. "I had seen her that night, you know…when she left your room. She was tiptoeing downstairs and smiling to herself like the cat who ate the canary."

"You did?" Preston turned to Guy. "You never said

anything."

"I am no tattletale." Guy raked his fingers through his curly hair and then glanced at Walter's plate. "Give me that, I am hungry."

Walter smirked. "You are always hungry. Lucky for you, there is enough to share."

"Okay guys," Preston said glancing at the clock. "It's nearly five o'clock in the morning in Dubai. Jordan should be awake."

"I'll call," Saint said dialing the number on his cell phone. "I can't call Case though he is at a concert. He'll be pissing mad that he missed this."

They stood around when Jordan came on the phone, and they said their hellos.

Guy lamented the fact that he couldn't show him his latest crop of giant strawberries. Saint wanted to confirm that he would be in Jamaica in time for the tux fittings. Walter wanted to know if he could come over for a vacation before Jordan left Dubai for good.

Preston watched them gratefully and with a sense of pride. They had a deeper brotherly bond than the norm. He figured it was because they had been through a lot when they were younger.

He could manage Pete on his own, but it was heartwarming to know that he had his brothers in his corner. They lived in the same townhouse complex. It was their complex; their other project after they had built the Wiley Business Center.

Jordan had thought it was a great idea to build three bedroom townhouses one for each brother in the same location in upper St. Andrew. It was a brilliant idea. Previously they had all been scattered around town, living in apartments.

This was more convenient, especially for Case and Jordan who was always traveling, Case didn't have to worry about someone feeding his cats—Walter kept them for him, and Jordan's place could be cleaned and aired out and his car serviced on a regular basis.

They mostly led their own lives, but it was hard not to be involved when you were so closely connected. He would have no shortage of babysitters for Pete.

It still had not connected with him that he was now an honest to goodness father. He figured that it would sink in soon.

It wasn't exactly a scary feeling. He already had a lot of responsibility in his young life, so it wasn't the responsibility that fazed him. It was just that he had always thought that he would do this the right way. He would find a woman that he loved, and then they would get married and then maybe two years later have children, maybe three or four.

"Preston?" Saint snapped him out of his reverie, "Aren't you going to tell Jordan?"

"Yes er..." Preston moved closer to the phone. "He is mine."

And then the questions started and he had to tell them Pete's story and then answer the inevitable question. "What are we going to do with him?"

"Keep him, of course," Preston said firmly. "I have Kyle Jones working on it. He said I would have to adopt Pete legally. I already contacted the home he ran away from to tell them he is fine. Kyle is handling the rest of the legalities with the administrators from the home. We were appointed a social worker. We'll meet with her tomorrow."

"So you have to adopt your own kid?" Jordan whistled, "why?"

"Because he belongs to the state. I have no legal rights to him at this point. Which means when I meet with that social worker I'll have to be vetted."

"Don't worry about that, you weren't half bad as a parental figure when I was growing up," Saint said. "If Case were here we could tell the social worker what an awesome big brother/parent you were to him. He was about Pete's age when you took care of him by yourself."

Jordan cleared his throat.

"And you too Jordy." Saint chuckled. "You two made growing up for us quite a unique experience. Remember when I was suspended from school for sneaking off campus to go fishing? You guys frightened me into taking the whole school thing seriously."

"I didn't mind them as pretend parents," Guy made a face, "but I dearly and I mean dearly missed my mother in the early days. Probably even more than dad. All boys need a mother, the feminine touch is important. I would not be as awkward around females now if I grew up with a woman."

"I am not awkward around females." Saint snorted. "Speak for yourself, Guy Wiley."

"Because they throw themselves at you so much that you are jaded." Walter snickered. "From the very old to the very young, they look at you, and your green eyes and swoon like you are some exotic rare male species, just because of the green eyes."

"And the body," Guy muttered, "You can't forget, the body. He looks good. I can't get my puny muscles to look anything like that."

Walter chuckled. "Can I tell you how shocked I am that out of all of us Saint is the one getting married first? You are just twenty-four, and she is twenty, what's the rush?"

"I love her." Saint shrugged, "why wait until I am old and gray. I'll never love anybody else like I love her. I don't want anybody else but her."

"Aww," Jordan said over the phone, "makes me feel a little

jealous."

"You don't have to be jealous," Walter growled, "what are you and Shawn dancing around each other for? Everybody knows that the both of you are more than friends. How can you be just friends with someone who finishes your sentences, loves everything you do and looks like a supermodel and acts like a warrior princess? Shawn is the perfect girl. If she was interested in me, I would give you some competition."

Jordan snorted. "We will not discuss Shawn and compete in the same breath. You must be crazy to even think it. There will be no competition over any woman among us. Never."

"Okay, okay" Walter laughed. "I know to back off when I hear your disapproving voice."

"Shawn and Jordan are not the topic right now, guys," Guy said looking at Preston. "Let's discuss Preston's convoluted love life."

They all turned to him.

"That boy is going to need a mother," Guy said cheekily, "Growing up without one was no fun for me. I want what is best for my nephew."

"You kill me," Preston muttered and sat on a stool. "It's not as if I have a prospective mother sitting around waiting for a newly discovered son. I broke up with Jaylee six months ago."

"Because she wanted marriage and commitment." Walter shook his head. "Has it ever occurred to you that you are screwed up? All of us are screwed up because of our parents and their relationship. We are all searching for perfect."

"And I found it," Saint said smugly, "and that is why I am not wasting a minute marrying Sandrene."

"Everybody searches for perfect." Preston snorted, "it's not just us. Everybody wants to be sure that they have made the right choice before they make the ultimate commitment.

Jaylee was not the right person for me. We both knew it, and it was an amicable parting of ways. No drama. I hate drama."

"Also a legacy that we all share," Walter murmured, "We know what happens when your life is filled with too much drama."

"You need to find Sheryl," Guy said biting into one of his strawberries. "If she is not institutionalized, which is the worst case scenario or already married and has a family, who knows, you both can find your way back to each other."

"She gave away her son for adoption," Saint groaned, "She might not want to have her past rearing its ugly head in her life now. I think you shouldn't try to find her. Don't look for her; you might be tempted to contact her. Let her be."

"No, don't listen to him," Guy frowned, "what if she is eating garbage from the street or she is living in a tenement yard? We should offer her some assistance."

"Assistance yes," Saint nodded, "but telling her about her child or even contemplating a relationship is a big no."

"What about Miss Pam?" Preston frowned. "It would be nice to find out what is going on with her."

"No!" Saint snorted. "They gave him away when he was a baby. They obviously had no intention of seeing him again. Besides, you'd be tempted to confess. 'Oh Miss Pam, remember that child that Sheryl had, turns out that I am the father.' If Sheryl is still crazy, you won't want her to know where you live."

Preston spread his arms wide." You may be right but..."

"But nothing," Walter said, "Saint is right, Call this a blessing that God brought your son to you. You now have a chance to right a wrong that you had done years ago. And then move along."

"Be the best father you can be," Jordan said over the phone.

Preston had forgotten that he was listening.

"And if the time comes when you meet someone who you can see yourself spending the rest of your life with, make sure she loves him as well before you marry her. The kid has already been through enough without stepmother drama."

"I will have to think about that," Preston said.

A little piece of him was extremely curious about what had happened to Sheryl. Maybe he wouldn't tell her that he had found their son. Maybe he just wanted to know what was happening with her. Maybe she too needed his help. Maybes...A lot of maybes were swirling in his head.

"He is going to still look for Sheryl," Jordan said resigned. "I can practically hear his thoughts from here."

Saint chuckled. "You two have always been unnaturally in tuned with each other."

"Shut up," Jordan growled. "I am going to get ready for work. I can't wait to come back home. You guys are falling apart without me."

"You wish." Walter chuckled. "Just admit that you miss us."

Preston listened to their banter absentmindedly. His mind was whirring. Should he or shouldn't he look for Sheryl?

There was no harm in looking for her. He didn't have to speak to her.

Chapter Five

"**A**re you listening to me?" Maci asked squinting over her glasses.

"Yes," Sheryl nodded, "you said Jamaica and then a little scream erupted in my head."

"Why?" Maci frowned. "Everybody who we've told that Carragon Suppliers will be operating in Jamaica practically begged me to go. They want to be on the list."

Sheryl sighed. "I don't have very good memories of Jamaica when I was younger. I used to live there, you know?"

"I know that you are from there," Maci smiled smugly, "and that is why you are on the top of my of persons to send to the island. Apart from that, you are the second top performer this quarter. The top two get an automatic add to the list."

Sheryl widened her eyes. Did she have to go? Couldn't she stage a protest and insist on staying or just quit?

She knew the answer to that, and it depressed her. She

couldn't just walk away from her position at Carragon Ltd. She was bonded to them.

They had paid her school fees, and in return, she had to work for them for three years. She had just gone a year out of that three, so she had two more to go. The company sponsored two persons every year to get their degrees. Now she wished she hadn't signed up for the degree program and completed it.

She wished she had just stuck with that high school diploma that she had eventually gotten after many years of trying. Concentration and school work went hand in hand, and she had been a wreck weaning herself off her psychiatric medication.

Luckily, she hadn't needed much concentration to be a salesperson, and she was one of the best salespersons that Carragon had in the region, they were a personal care supplier, and she had consistently and continuously sold more items than any other sales person even while doing college.

Sales was her thing. She could sell anything; her natural shyness disappeared when she was pushing a product. She was in second place now, but as soon as Journey Stores sent in their invoice, she would be back on top. She had gotten them to start carrying Carragon's makeup brands, and that was for eleven stores!

She couldn't go to Jamaica. She had almost finished saving to buy her own place. It would be a huge relief to move out from her aunt's basement flat. She was so close to leaving. She had a picture of the house she was eying taped to her wall. She looked at it every night and thanked God for already providing it for her.

Moving out of the San Francisco area was a no-no. Moving to Jamaica was a hell no! She knew that Carragon had recently acquired a retail supplies business in the Caribbean. She had heard the rumors; they had bought out a company with a large warehouse and offices. She had no idea that the Caribbean meant Jamaica or that she would be asked to go.

"How did this happen, so fast?" Sheryl asked out loud, "I only just heard about this Caribbean venture."

"It has been in the pipeline for about a year," Maci said. "They bought out the company that was distributing our products in that region. The previous company was not doing such a good job down there. The Carragon management team thinks that they could have had a bigger share of the Caribbean market if our own people were at the wheel."

"The reason you haven't heard about it is the same reason you rarely hear anything much. It's because we are just sales. They always take us for granted even though we are the backbone of this company."

Sheryl settled in her chair for the familiar complaint. Maci was not just a sales manager. She was married to the brother of the owner of the company. She was family, not one of the regular employees. The whole sales team found her 'Them and Us' speeches hilarious.

Sheryl sat patiently while Maci did her diatribe.

"Anyway," Maci said after Sheryl was just about to go cross-eyed.

"Noel Paul will be heading up the company out there. I hope it won't be a problem since you two...er...have history."

Sheryl groaned. Exactly one year ago Noel had proposed to her and then she had blabbed about her past. She hadn't even told him everything, and he had dumped her like a sack of hot potatoes. He had not even done it face to face. He had done it via text.

I am sorry Sheryl. I am not the type of man that can handle baggage like yours. I chose you because you seemed different and normal. How do I know that your mental health issues won't come up again? I can't take the chance of you having a relapse and then trying to kill me or worse sleeping with everybody on the apartment block. I am sorry.

PS can you return the ring? It was my grandmother's and a very expensive diamond.

"Noel Paul, peachy, just peachy," Sheryl murmured.

"I know you have both moved on," Maci said oblivious to her unease. "He is now engaged, and you are...erm...single which is another reason you were top of this list, you have no ties...A change of scenery is just what you need Sheryl. Please don't make me choose anyone else. You are perfect for this. You can always come back after you have trained a couple of the locals."

"Training?" Sheryl straightened in her chair. "I would have to do training sessions?"

"Yes, in conjunction with HR," Maci nodded, "just three six weeks sessions per year. We have the material. It's not like you would have to prepare anything. And your base pay is going to get a serious bump for this. Your job title will be senior sales representative."

Maci slid a paper across the desk. "This is the offer and your responsibilities."

"I have to do this for two years?" Sheryl looked at Maci in horror. "Two years in Jamaica?"

"If you like, it could be longer as we expand in the Caribbean," Maci said hopefully, "Did you see the base salary?"

"I did," Sheryl swallowed, "I am just..." she massaged her temples. She had vowed never to go back to Jamaica. She had too many bad memories there. It was as if God was working against her. She had plans; everything was finally lining up her way. She was finally and totally off her medications and was feeling normal. She hadn't felt normal in years. And now this...

"Sleep on it," Maci said giving her one of her less than sincere smiles. She was not pleased, it was obvious. She had probably expected Sheryl to jump at the opportunity for change.

She didn't know that Sheryl hated changes especially changes like this.

"When would I be expected to go?" Sheryl asked belatedly.

"February twelfth." Maci's expression became animated again. "HR is already down there, and they have accommodation worked out. You get a nice apartment, which is very close to the new office, and a company car."

Sheryl winced. "February twelfth is in five weeks!"

"Which is a whole thirty-five days!" Maci said sweetly. "HR needs your travel details so that they can arrange your itinerary. Don't be a spoiled puss, Sheryl. This is a wonderful adventure, and I know you will do exceptionally well. You are one of the best sales personnel Carragon has."

****

Don't be a spoiled puss! Sheryl mumbled all the way home from the Financial District to Nob Hill. She was never spoiled. She had never been spoiled in her life!

She got looks from people on the bus as she fumed.

Spoiled Puss! Never! More like a fraidy puss. Nobody wanted to revisit the most embarrassing place in their lives.

She didn't have many memories of the two years when she was certifiably insane, just broken nightmares that she was never sure were real or imagined.

She didn't even remember much of her pregnancy. She had been hospitalized and on drugs. Going back would be stressful, and Maci had the nerve to call her spoiled puss.

But Sheryl would never breathe a word about it to Maci; she didn't talk about it to anyone outside of her family. She had therapy for years, and she had let it all out. And what was more she was off medication.

She could concentrate like the rest of the population and make rational decisions; her brain chemicals were back to normal.

She was a rational, self-aware human being, who didn't have random, uncontrollable sexual urges but she didn't want to go back to Jamaica.

Through the years she had avoided everything Jamaican like the plague. She pretended as if the country did not exist. It was her way of coping.

She let herself into her apartment, kicked off her shoes, and contemplated calling her grandmother or her aunt Lena but definitely not her mom. Her mother also had her attitude about Jamaica; she didn't like to be reminded of their dark days.

Pamela didn't even like to talk about the days before the dark days. The days before the accident.

She had told the therapist in one of their family sessions that she felt guilty whenever she thought about that time and how naive she was in not getting Sheryl the help she needed in time before the pregnancy.

Pamela still blamed herself for everything and point blank refused to talk about any of it outside of therapy sessions.

She had remarried ten years ago to an organic farmer, Jasper Santiago. He ran a bed and breakfast and organic farming outfit in Southern California. Pamela had promptly changed her surname from Stone to Santiago and had completely moved on from her past life. Needless to say, her least favorite topics, in no particular order were: teenage pregnancy, adoptions, mental health problems and Jamaica.

Her grandmother and her aunt, Lena were available to talk though. They loved their island home. It held no bad memories for them

Her aunt Lena was especially fond of Jamaica because she had recently met a hunky Rasta man there after her second divorce and was planning to go back to "Live with him in his Rasta commune in the hills of St Andrew until the passion ran out." Her words.

Passion. Sex. Sheryl had repressed that side of herself for years. Her therapist said she was operating from a place of guilt, but Sheryl did not think so.

She was just not attracted to anyone. Two years ago she had thought that she was attracted to Noel Paul. It was pathetic how excited she had been to feel something for someone. She had thought that the medication and the therapy from her teen years had rendered her uninterested in anything remotely sexual.

It was also pathetic how eager she was to tell him about her past when he had proposed. They had been at dinner at his house. She was in a maroon-red dress. It was one that showed a bit of cleavage. He was in a white dress shirt and black pants; his hair slicked back. He had looked handsome in the half-light. He was a mixed-race man; both his parents were biracial. His mother was Asian and White. His father was black and Indian. He had the best of all the ethnicities combined: slightly slanted gray eyes, dark olive toned skin, thick wavy black hair, and perfect bone structure.

She had cupped her hand under her chin admiring him as he talked and laughed about something at work. He was the head of the Marketing and Sales Division at Carragon, which technically meant he was her boss.

Well, she had two bosses before him: Maci and Kelly. Maci was the one who had introduced them at a Christmas party. It had taken off from there. She had been fascinated by the fact that he didn't drink or smoke and spoke proudly about being in his church choir.

But that particular night, his gray eyes were focused on her as if she was the only woman in the world and she had liked that, loved it even. She had found herself wondering how on earth she had gotten so lucky to have him interested in her. He was perfect.

And then he had leaned in and kissed her, deeper with more passion than he had previously exhibited and then he had asked, Sheryl will you marry me?

She had said yes. Of course, she had. This was a blessing. She was finally off her medications and feeling normal. This was her reward.

And then she had confessed, "Noel, there is something that you should know."

"What is it?" He had pulled away from her slightly.

"I had some issues when I was younger. You see, I met in an accident while I was riding my bike and I damaged my head, lost my inhibitions for a while, and I suffered from hypersexuality."

"Hypersexuality?" The distance between them on the couch had grown wider; she should have known that she should shut up after that.

"You acted on it?" His voice was sharper than usual.

"I did." Sheryl nodded, "I can't remember much of that time, but I do remember that I was pregnant at fifteen."

His gasp was strong.

"I know, shocking huh?" Sheryl had said nervously. "My mom gave my child up for adoption. I don't remember much about the birth or anything like that."

"You have a child?" Noel had visibly shuddered.

"Had a child. Biologically." Her voice had gotten

defensive. "Obviously, I don't have him with me. I was mentally unstable at the time."

"Mentally unstable!" Noel had looked frightened. "Are you on medication?"

"Not anymore," Sheryl had proudly declared. "I gradually came off. It was tough for a while."

"So you don't have the urge to drop your clothes for the nearest male anymore?" Noel had asked waspishly.

"No." Sheryl had felt let down by his mockery.

"Who was the kid's father? "Noel had gotten up and started pacing.

"I don't know," Sheryl had said her voice low, she had felt like crying at the question. The truth was that she had beaten up herself with that question over the years. She did not have the vaguest recollection about most of that time.

Her mother said the fake doctor who was supposed to have helped her had raped her. Dr. Sam Fay. She barely remembered the man.

She wished she could remember but who wanted to remember rape. Besides, she was probably the one who had pursued him and that she definitely did not want to recall.

"My God." Noel had stopped and looked at her shocked. "I can't marry a slut. I thought I knew you, but this is too much."

"But, I haven't been with anybody since then. I only ended up that way because of an accident. Please understand."

"I can't." Noel had shaken his head, "I don't want to marry a mentally unstable person who gave away her child and doesn't even know who the father is. I imagine it was a long list of candidates."

"I honestly don't know." Her voice had been hoarse with tears. "I don't have any sexually transmitted diseases though. I just thought you should know..."

"Get out!" Noel had screamed. "Get out of this house now. Right now!"

He had practically pushed her out of the house with the ring on her finger too. She had returned it the next day after she had gotten Noel's rotten text. The official break-up text in writing.

Sheryl sprawled out on her futon and looked up at her ceiling. And now Noel was going to be her immediate boss in the country where it all went sour.

Could she go back? Yes, she could.

Could she hold her curiosity at bay and not go searching for the son she gave away? Yes, she could.

Did she want to search for him? Oh God yes. It had plagued her through the years. Of course, she couldn't admit it out loud to anyone, least of all her mother who had told her the last time she had floated the idea, that she should let sleeping dogs lie.

She dreamed about him. She liked to imagine that he was happy and well taken care of and was better off without her but she wasn't sure that was true and that sometimes made her sad.

She wished that she hadn't given him up. She hoped that she could have a second chance. Maybe going back would be her second chance, but how?

She had no clue where her son would be. Her mother had handled all the details. She had not been in her right mind at the time and worse she had been underage.

She picked up the phone to call her mother and then changed her mind. She was not in the mood to hear her mother burst out crying and accusing her of dwelling unnecessarily in the past.

She probably would get around to it and maybe she would not. She did not have the energy to tackle her mother about it and she never would. Maybe going to Jamaica was not a bad idea after all.

The only drawback she could foresee was working with Noel Paul. He was not going to be an easy boss to work with. Even though he was the one who broke up with her, he still treated her as if she had done something to him.

And what about the Wiley's? Preston to be exact, what had happened to them? She had often wondered through the years. Had the boys split up?

But she wouldn't go looking for them, they had seen her at her worst, and she didn't want to associate with anybody who had known her like that. That chapter of her life was closed.

Done with.

Never to be reopened.

Chapter Six

God had a sense of humor. Preston thought darkly as he sat across from Jaylee who was regarding him with barely held together rage.

"You are my twelve o'clock appointment?" She all but screeched the question. "You have a son? What kind of nonsense is this Preston? I am a social worker, not a time waster. If you wanted to see me to rekindle our relationship, one call would have done it. Not this elaborate ruse. I do have other pressing matters to deal with, you know!"

Preston cleared his throat. Of all the social workers to assign to work on his case. They had to send Jaylee.

"Don't go," he sighed, "he is in Walter's office. Let me ask Walter to bring him in."

"You have a son? For real?" Jaylee frowned, "but when did this happen...I never knew you did I?"

"You knew me well enough," Preston said gently, "we just never gelled."

He shouldn't have said that. Jaylee glared at him. If her stare could kill, he would be dead.

"You are a commitment-phobe with a thousand and one hang-ups about relationships, but you are right, we never gelled. I want to marry someone who isn't so neurotic about everything."

"I am not neurotic." Preston sighed, "just an overly cautious guy who didn't grow up with the best example of what a normal relationship should be, so it makes me picky."

He picked up the phone and called Walter while Jaylee picked up her briefcase and pulled out a sheaf of papers.

He asked Walter to bring Pete in and then hung up the phone.

"Are you sure he is yours?" Jaylee asked sullenly, "you must have been pretty young when he was conceived."

"I was sixteen," Preston said. "We did a DNA test this morning. The results will be available by the end of the week."

A brief knock on the door interrupted their conversation and Walter walked in with Pete.

Walter widened his eyes when he saw Jaylee and then decided to try his hand at damage control.

"Hi, Jaylee. It's nice to know Preston has an old friend working on this case."

Jaylee wasn't listening to Walter she stared at Pete and then blinked her eyes.

"My God, he is yours!"

"I'll leave you three to it." Walter let himself out of the office.

Jaylee got up. She was a curvy and petite woman with flawless dark-brown skin tone and short curly hair, which she wore in a pixie cut. Her best feature was her lips; they were bow shaped with the bottom ones more generous than the top. When she wasn't sneering at him, she looked like a cute imp who was on the verge of laughter.

He had met her on the shop floor a year ago when he had been doing his rounds in the supermarket. She had been a regular shopper who had been dithering about which cream to get for a strawberry and cream dessert.

Strawberries had been on sale from Guy's farm, and she had stocked up on them and was super excited about trying them out.

He was attracted to her. Maybe it was her smile or her zest for life that had drawn him. Whatever it was, he had gone over to her and proceeded to help her choose the best cream.

A few months into dating Jaylee he had realized that something was missing. She was still the same bubbly warm woman who would make some man very happy but not him.

He started distancing himself from her when she started talking about getting married and having children. He had explained to her that he had to be sure about marrying someone before he made a move. That's what she called his neurosis. Maybe he was a bit neurotic but who wouldn't be after their mother killed their father because he dared to leave her for someone he loved. He had no intention of having that sort of history repeating itself in his life.

He needed to commit to someone who had all the right options ticked in his head.

He looked over at Jaylee. She was standing in front of Pete they were almost at the same height. Pete was going to be tall. He could see that already.

He picked up the phone to call Helena; they needed to get Pete some new clothes, a whole wardrobe. He ate like a starving refugee, so Preston would have to stock up on groceries and snacks and figure out a way to get him into private school. Helena's sister was principal of a private prep school.

When he was near Pete's age, he had met Jordan for the first time. It was kind of hard to imagine a time when Jordan wasn't in his life or Guy or Case.

He had been twenty years old when Case was twelve; all five of them had taken Case to his first day of high school. Case had solemnly told them to back off; they were cramping his style.

Preston suppressed a chuckle; he was familiar with little boys and their quest for independence. He had been the same, and this son of his had a touch more than he should. He had survived on the street for four months, moving from one section of the island to the other and using his resilience to stay alive.

He had the Wiley genes in him all right.

Preston wished that he had known him as a baby, but they couldn't have taken him on. It was no use wishing for the impossible now.

"Boss," Helena said in his ear. "You are silent."

"Oh." Preston looked down at the phone and stated his requests to Helena.

"Clothes, school and food," Helena said, "that can be arranged, especially the food, you do own a supermarket, and my sister would probably do cartwheels when she hears that you are interested in enrolling your son in her school— you are after all their favorite donor."

Preston chuckled. "Somehow, I can't imagine the very reserved Carlene Channer doing cartwheels."

Preston hung up the phone and watched, as Jaylee and Pete were still deep in conversation.

Jaylee walked over to the desk and sat down. Pete came behind her reluctantly.

"What did you say to him?" Preston asked, looking at

Pete's hangdog expression.

"I told him the truth, he belongs to me for the time being," Jaylee said briskly, "However, I will make a recommendation for temporary custody. I will check on you every two weeks for the next couple of weeks."

She then turned to Pete and smiled at him sweetly. "Pete could you excuse me for a while; I need to speak to your father for just a moment."

Pete nodded. "I am going to uncle Walter's office."

Preston nodded. "That's fine."

Jaylee watched him go and then turned to Preston. "He is a handsome boy—Very polite and sweet. Whoever had him before this must have been a stickler for propriety."

"I realized that," Preston said. "He is pretty amazing."

"You love him already." Jaylee smiled, but it didn't reach her eyes.

"I do," Preston said. "It's hard to explain the kind of emotions that are running through me right now. I am looking forward to getting to know him and watch him grow up."

"That's very nice," Jaylee said briskly, "I am assuming that you want to legally adopt him?"

"Yes." Preston nodded.

"You have to make an application." Jaylee crossed her legs and did her best schoolmarm expression. "If your application is approved you will be assigned a case worker to check your home for its suitability."

Preston nodded. "I thought as much."

"After all documentation required is obtained, all consents and interviews gathered, your application will be ready for the Case Committee, and a report prepared and submitted to the Adoption Board for approval."

Preston frowned. "Really?"

"That's not all; we don't just give away children in

this country." Jaylee sneered, "They are not commodity. The Adoption Board will make a decision, and the Case Committee will inform you of the outcome. If you are approved, then comes court. The court is the one who has to make an adoption legal with a court order."

"Wow," Preston groaned. "How long will this take?"

"Four months… up to a year. You can be refused as well. You are not entitled to this child just because he is biologically yours," Jaylee said maliciously, "besides if there is someone on the Case Committee or the Adoption Board that doesn't think you are suitable, that person can stall, or delay, this adoption or simply make your life hell."

Preston straightened up in his chair, "which one of them are you on?"

"The Adoption Board." Jaylee chuckled wickedly. "Yes Preston, you had better be nice to me, or your precious little boy is going straight back to the foster system."

Preston tapped the desk. "What exactly do you mean by be 'nice' to you?"

"Let's get married, have our own kids. Pete will have some brothers and sisters and a mother, and it will show that you have some stability."

Preston looked at Jaylee and then started to laugh. "You know that my mother did something very similar to my father and that she ended up killing him and the woman that he loved and then herself on my birthday when I was thirteen years old?"

Jaylee opened her mouth. "What?"

"I don't do blackmail." Preston shook his head. "I don't love you, Jay. The truth is, you are a nice person, well I thought you were until this conversation, but I won't be blackmailed into anything. Not even for Pete's sake."

Jaylee looked at him crossly. "I wasn't blackmailing you.

I just want to jerk you out of your anti commitment stupor. Did your mother kill your father for real?"

"Yes." Preston nodded. "He didn't love her. He loved his childhood sweetheart, and he had no intentions of leaving his love, and that made my mother maddeningly jealous."

"So you have madness in your family?" Jaylee glared at him, "that is good to know. I will just have to bring that up at the board meeting."

Preston forced himself not to react. Even though he wanted to shout, *No! You are the one that is crazy!* He had no idea that Jaylee had been so invested in their relationship that she would do something like this. He had thought that they had parted ways amicably.

He didn't know much about women, did he? Maybe in her twisted way Jaylee was right about him not being a suitable parent for Pete, the boy probably needed female guidance in his life.

Preston had gotten precious little in his teenage years. But he wasn't that worse off. Would he have been better off with a mother? His own mother? Probably not.

"I will tell them that you are a womanizing stinker with a fear of commitment. That's bad you know, especially if you want to take care of a child. Children are a lifetime commitment." Jaylee got up and smirked. "You have my number, and you know where to reach me. I'll be coming to your home to see you in two weeks. I will give you a call when I want to drop by."

She stormed out of his office, and Preston sat in his chair stunned. He quickly called Kyle who confirmed that there could be delays in the adoption process if someone along the way made trouble for him.

"Would it be better if I am married?" Preston asked hesitantly.

"Oh yes," Kyle said. "Fair or not, single people do get a lot more scrutiny than a couple would; that is just the way it is, but I don't think you have to worry you have a biological connection to the boy, that is usually a plus."

No, it wasn't, Preston thought after he hung up the phone. Not if mad Jaylee was hell-bent on making trouble for him.

Chapter Seven

Three weeks later.

Preston did not allow Jaylee's threats to dampen his relationship with his son. He was enjoying getting to know Pete. For the past two weeks, they had settled into a routine that seemed to be working. He left for the office at eight in the morning. He dropped Pete off at the school.

His housekeeper, Blossom, picked him up from the school at three. And then Preston was home by five to hang out with Pete. They played tennis together at the home court, or they swam in the pool. Sometimes one or more of his brothers joined them. It was all in an effort to get to know Pete better and to get him settled into his new life.

Pete was a gregarious boy and was easy to relate to. Preston was glad that Pete hadn't inherited his personality. It would have been harder to get to know him if he were as quiet and introspective as he was.

Instead, Pete asked a lot of questions, and he shared what

he was thinking, that made him easier to relate to.

Guy and Walter came over for dinner and dominoes, and Pete had them in stitches relating stories about his time at school. He had already made friends and was pretty sanguine about his new situation. Preston had unnecessarily fretted that he was introducing him to too much all at once, but Pete was taking it all in stride. He had a small class of friendly prep schoolers who had accepted him as easily as children that age did without an issue.

"My teacher, Miss Fallon says that she went to school with you, Daddy," Pete said looking across at him.

"Summer B Fallon." Preston smiled. "Yes, she did. She was something else."

"Her name is still Miss Fallon?" Walter asked curiously. "I must visit your school to throw my uncle weight around."

Guy laughed. "You had a crush on Summer when you were going to Titchfield High?"

"Everybody had a crush on Summer," Walter murmured, "And now she is a teacher. I bet she gets more presents than the others on Teacher's Day."

Preston laughed. "I never had a crush on Summer, I eventually grew to like her, but my initial thoughts of her was that she was...er...too...inquisitive."

"Why?" Pete put down his dominoes; he loved to hear about his father and uncle's past. He found it amazing that they grew up without parents. He was also patiently waiting to hear who his biological mother was. He was somehow afraid to ask because he didn't want to hear bad news. He was low key thinking that she was dead.

"Well," Preston sighed, "it's a long story, but there was a time when the six Wiley brothers were not familiar with each other. I was twelve before I saw your uncle Jordan face to face."

"Our family situation was messed up," Walter murmured. "Your grandfather had two families."

"That's right," Preston said, "three boys in each family and we lived in the same area."

"Wow." Pete widened his eyes.

"Yes," Preston nodded, "my first encounter with Summer was her asking me about the situation. Your uncle Jordan and I look very much alike, and we were in the same class and yet had never spoken to each other… Summer wanted to find out why. I hated her questions. I was quite upset about it."

Preston sighed. "Through the years we became friendly. We lost touch after high school though. I am not surprised that she is a teacher."

"I am," Walter murmured. "I was thinking model."

"I was thinking a journalist or something in PR," Guy said, "or even advertising exec. Summer gave off that kind of vibe."

Walter shrugged. "You are right. I wasn't trying to objectify her. I just thought that she could give some of the so-called models these days a run for their money."

"Miss Fallon?" Pete asked incredulously, "I don't think we are talking about the same Miss Fallon."

"What?" Walter asked his mouth hanging open. "What happened to Summer?"

"She is going to have a baby soon. Well not one baby, two of them. Her belly is out to here." Pete extended his arms far across the table. "She might not be around next month."

Guy was the first to laugh. "There goes your fantasy of hitting on Summer B, Walter."

Walter sighed dramatically. "My heart, my wounded heart."

Preston and Guy snickered.

"My PE teacher Miss Jones doesn't have a belly," Pete said helpfully.

"Thank you for looking out, nephew." Walter winked at Pete, "but I think I will do any future meetings face to face, just in case."

Pete nodded solemnly.

"You should take Pete to Portland." Guy suggested, "Show him around."

"I will." Preston nodded. I was thinking of going over to the villa next weekend.

"The villa?" Pete widened his eyes.

Preston nodded. "Yes, I have a villa in Portland, and then we can take a tour of my old hangout spots."

****

Pete spent most of the drive over to Portland from Kingston with his mouth hanging open.

"So you lived here?" Pete asked him wide-eyed as he looked through the car window at the passing scenery.

"Yes." Preston nodded. "We all did. Your uncles and I grew up right here."

"It's nice. I like the sea," Pete said looking through the car window in excitement. "Can we go swimming?"

"Sure." Preston nodded. "The villa is pretty close to the water."

"Cool." Pete looked at him and grinned. "Why can't we live here, I prefer it to Kingston."

Preston smiled. "You can have the best of both; I come over here pretty often."

He slowed down at their Portland supermarket and pointed. "That was our second supermarket. "My mom and dad started it together. One day I'll tell you the story of how we lost it all and had to fight our way back."

Pete nodded solemnly.

"That's part of the reason why I let your mother go," Preston said regretfully. "I had nothing to offer her, and she was sick."

"I want to know more about her," Pete said tentatively. "I was a little afraid to ask."

"You don't have to be afraid to ask me anything." Preston glanced at him "Unfortunately, I have no clue what to tell you about her. I haven't seen or heard from her in years. What I do remember is that she was a beautiful girl with the prettiest mahogany eyes."

Preston smiled sadly. "And she was going places until she met in a horrible accident that messed with her head.

"Ah, there it is, our old house." Preston slowed down the car; it was now a boutique hotel. The black wrought iron gates were closed.

"You lived there?" Pete whispered the question. "It's huge."

Preston laughed. "Yep, that was where we lived."

He drove into the scheme a few meters from that house and stopped at their other house. Jackie had moved her salon to the town years ago.

It was funny, for Preston the nostalgia was particularly intense at this house. He had only started living here when he was sixteen, but this place was where he had really grown up, and so he considered it home.

He got out of the car and Pete followed him. They both stood at the gate. The yard was well kept, and the house was freshly painted. Jordan had a lady from the community clean it every week.

They had refused to rent it out even though they had their houses in Kingston; it just sat here for most of the year unlived in.

Case and Jordan stayed there when they returned to Portland; all the others had their villas.

"Where is this?" Pete asked.

"This is the house of memories." Preston looked at his son and then opened the gate. "Your uncles and I lived here after we lost everything."

"Cool. You lived alone?" Pete already knew the answer, but he wanted to confirm, "Without parents?"

"It wasn't all that exciting," Preston snorted, "the oldest boys, me and your uncle Jordan, had to act like parents and we had school and a business to get off the ground and a stubborn as a mule brother, your uncle Walter, to supervise."

Pete chuckled.

"We had all the grown-up things to do like pay bills and make sure that everybody was eating healthy, part fights, pacify quarrels and provide wise counsel. Six boys living together was not particularly frictionless. We had our moments."

"Guess which brother we had to convince to stop digging up the place to plant things?"

"Uncle Guy." Pete smiled. It was nearly a month; he was more than familiar with his uncles by now, except for Case and Jordan who were not around. He had spoken to them on the phone though.

Preston nodded. "Yep and then when Saint was about fourteen or so we had a girl problem."

"Girl problem?" Pete widened his eyes.

"We had girls camping out on the front lawn to see him. It was pretty annoying."

"Wow. Really?"

"Really." Preston smiled fondly at the memories. "We had to put in sprinklers on the lawn and turn them on. That solved the problem of them loitering around hoping to see him. I hope we won't have to resort to that with you."

Pete laughed. "I don't like any girl in particular, not yet."

"It's coming; it's a part of growing up." Preston opened the front door. It smelled like furniture polish and potpourri.

Preston walked through the rooms. He always checked on the house like an old familiar friend when he returned to Portland.

His next stop would be Pastor Tate's place. He had to introduce him to Pete. That would take a while and then to the villa he would go.

****

Pastor Tate Griffith and his wife Adalynn had not aged all that much in twelve years. They were shocked to meet Pete but recovered pretty quickly. Pete took to them like he had always known them and had developed an easy rapport with the pastor's children, Ava and Aiden. They were a few years older than he was.

Preston and Tate were sitting in the kitchen while Adalynn washed the dishes after supper.

Preston told them how he found out about Pete.

"God works in mysterious ways." Tate whistled. "I tell you, it's amazing."

Preston nodded. "That's what I thought."

"Have you tried to find Miss Pamela and Sheryl?" Adalynn asked.

"Yes. I hired a private investigator." Preston sighed, "My PI is fairly sure that they are not in Jamaica. He found where they previously lived in Kingston. That place was sold years ago. I am in this alone, and you know what? I don't mind."

"I wonder what became of Sheryl though," Adalynn said wistfully. "She was a lovely young lady. I hope she came out all right."

"I still pray for her," Tate said. "I am confident that she pulled through that time in her life and came out okay."

"I hope you find her," Adalynn said. "I have a good feeling about Sheryl."

Preston shook his head. "I try not to think about her. I am just grateful that she had my son and I found him after all this time. To waste time thinking about her now is fruitless."

Chapter Eight

Sheryl had a six-foot-one giant sized headache called Noel Paul. She had hardly set foot down on Jamaican soil and settled her luggage in the middle of the living room of the one bedroom apartment before her phone rang.

"We are having a staff meeting tomorrow at nine; I hope you can make it," Noel said he hadn't even greeted her, and he growled the request at her as if speaking to her was a particularly distasteful task.

"Er...yes, I can make it." Sheryl sank down on the sofa when she heard his voice. She had not encountered him much in a year, and whenever she did, he had always sounded slightly hostile. How were they going to work together?

It seemed as if they were thinking the same thing because Noel cleared his throat. "Do you want us to get a meal this evening and clear the air between us?"

She wanted to say no. She was tired, but they needed to talk. She was over him, but they needed to get their new working relationship sorted out. It could be done if they both worked at it.

"Sure," she said lightly, even though she was feeling anything but light.

"We could meet at the Pegasus; it's just a short walk over from where you are. Meet me at the Blue Window Restaurant. Tonight is Tuesday Night at the Grill. I heard from a colleague that their food is excellent. Meet me there at eight."

"Okay." Sheryl hung up the phone. She had a slight headache, and she would have liked to have a quiet night to unpack and get her bearings, but this was necessary, and she did have seven hours to grab a nap, have a shower, wash her hair, unpack and feel human again.

She also needed to get food.

She looked around her space. It was a lovely apartment. It was fully furnished in a black and white theme and decorated with zebra rugs, white walls, black settees and accompanying white lamps. She was on the third floor. The living room and kitchen were spacious and the patio door opened to a view of another building—the Pegasus hotel she assumed.

She turned on the music system and tried to find a station that played music nonstop. She stopped when she heard Roberta Flack's, Summertime. It was one of her favorite songs. She turned up the volume and nodded her head all the way to the bedroom. It too was also tastefully done in the black and white theme. She was going to be comfortable in this space.

She headed to the en-suite bathroom and glanced at herself in the mirror. She wasn't looking too shabby these days. She had mastered the art of shaping up her thick eyebrows. It had taken her years to perfect the technique, but they were looking like perfect arches above her clear brown eyes.

Preston had been fascinated with her eyes. He had called them mahogany.

The thought came out of nowhere, and she shut it down. She focused once more on her face. She had a spot on her right cheek from a wayward zit, but that would soon fade. Apart from that, her complexion was so clear that she didn't bother with much makeup these days. Her eat clean, exercise and drink plenty of water regime was doing wonders for her skin. It had been important to be obsessively healthy after coming off her psychiatric medication. It was nice to know that it had paid off skin-wise.

Her hair needed attention though. She had not given it much care during the past two weeks. She had it pulled back in a no-fuss bun for most of the time. Tonight it deserved to be washed and let out of prison. It was a mass of dense, tight curls that reached a little past her waist when stretched. She applied henna to it every month, and now it had a distinct and dramatic burgundy tint.

She was going to look good tonight. She contemplated wearing a green halter-top dress to show off her toned arms. She was going to make Noel Paul eat his disdain of her. She was going to make him regret sending her that dear Jane text, breaking their engagement, calling her a slut and almost sending her back into a funk.

And she was going to work with him and be as cordial as she could, but she purposed never to discuss her past with a man again.

She had learned her lesson.

****

She walked into the hotel lobby, and people stared. It filled her with confidence and gave her a little extra pep in her step.

From the entrance to the restaurant, she could hear a live

steel band playing and get a clear view of the pool and the tables, through the windows. Though the interior of the restaurant was not crowded, she could see that the outside tables were occupied.

She spotted Noel at a table that had a good view of the door. He waved to her at the same time a hostess came over to her.

She was ushered to Noel's poolside table. The night was balmy, and the temperature was right. She was thankful that they were not seated inside the restaurant.

Noel was staring at her. He couldn't quite keep his mouth closed.

"Good evening," Sheryl said to him sweetly, "I am famished. I tried not to snack before I got here."

"Yes, it is a good evening," Noel whistled. "Wow, you look...amazing."

"Thank you," Sheryl said briskly. He didn't look too bad himself in his white open-necked shirt and jacket and blue jeans, but she was not going to tell him that. "Something smells good here."

"It's the grill. I had a kebab while I waited." Noel nodded to a hovering waiter who took their orders. Sheryl got lamb cutlets, and Noel got salmon fillet.

"Thank you for joining me." Noel cleared his throat. "I thought you wouldn't have come."

Sheryl shrugged. "Whatever happened between us happened over a year ago. I know we have to work closely, it would be pointless to hold a grudge."

"I was a bigoted pig." Noel held her gaze. "I have no excuse for how I reacted when you told me about your past. And that letter, I wrote it in a fog. I was just so angry that..."

"I wasn't the ideal that you had in your head. I understand." Sheryl nodded. "I get it. People fear what they don't know, and mental illness is a no-go area for many people. I just thought that if you are planning to spend the rest of your life with someone, then certain information should not be withheld."

"That's true." Noel sighed. "I confessed to Crystal that I still had feelings for you and we broke it off before I moved out here. "

"How sad," Sheryl said dispassionately. She settled back in her chair, "I don't have any feelings for you, not anymore."

Noel nodded. "I get it. I do. I just wanted to clear the air and to reassure you that I will not be treating you any differently from the rest of the team. We are colleagues, plain and simple. Maybe one day..."

He looked at her expression and held up his hand. "Okay, all is completely lost. I completely blew it. I get it now."

Sheryl was relieved when the waiter brought their starters. And she was doubly relieved when Noel started talking about business.

"You are the last of the sales team to arrive from head office. We have our work cut out for us, penetrating the Caribbean market, but it's doable."

Sheryl nodded. "And exciting."

"The research team has done their due diligence, most of the major retailers have head offices in Kingston. I hope you are not too tired from your flight because you are going to have to hit the ground running tomorrow."

"I am fine. I am up for it." Sheryl smiled. "I always meet my quota."

"Do you still have family here?" Noel asked. "I never thought to ask that before."

"No, I..." Sheryl paused and looked by the door.

It couldn't be him, Preston Wiley. It was just a coincidence.

She focused on Noel and then looked at the door again. *It*

was him. Who could mistake that caramel complexion and those hooded eyes? He was clean-shaven, even his head, and he was tall. *Goodness.* He had gotten taller and even better looking than when they were young. The boy was now a man. A very handsome man.

A little nervous flutter started in her heart region, and she dragged her eyes from him and back to Noel.

"Somebody, you know?" Noel asked raising an eyebrow.

"I think so." Sheryl looked down at her plate.

"He wasn't one of your..." Noel bit his lip, "Sorry."

"I shouldn't have told you." Sheryl closed her eyes and then opened them again. "I should have just kept my mouth shut."

"I am sorry." Noel looked uncomfortable. "I just...I think it. I wonder you know. I am only human. This is where you had your problems and..."

"Please," Sheryl cut him off, "is it even remotely possible that we can work together?"

"Yes, of course." Noel nodded. "This is a small lapse. I am an idiot. I am sorry I brought it up."

Sheryl eagerly looked toward the door again, but Preston was no longer there. He was seated on the inside with a mixed group of people: three males, two females. She had no way of telling if he was with someone special. A lady was sitting beside him, but she looked older.

Maybe he now likes older women.

And why did she care? She didn't. She focused on Noel once more and only glanced over at Preston five times that night.

The fifth time, he caught her looking. He was talking to the guy to his right, and then he looked at her through the glass. Their eyes caught and held.

A little frown of puzzlement formed between his eyes but

then the gentleman to his left said something to him, and he looked around, the spell was broken.

She hurriedly got up. "I am going to have to go if I am to hit the ground running tomorrow."

Noel looked at her contemplatively and then nodded. "What goes on in that pretty head of yours?"

"Nothing that should concern you overly," Sheryl hissed, goodnight. "Thanks for dinner."

"See you tomorrow," Noel said. "I will just stay here and finish up my dinner."

****

Sheryl arrived at work ten minutes late the next morning. It wasn't exactly an auspicious start to her first day, but she had the greatest difficulty falling asleep the night before and when she did she dreamt about long forgotten memories from her childhood.

She was racing on her bike with Shawn, Preston, and Jordan. She wondered where Shawn was now. She had gotten up in the middle of the night wondering about where they were now and what they were doing.

And then in the wee hours of the morning, she had a very erotic dream of her and Preston. She had walked into his room naked and got under the sheets with him.

For the life of her, she couldn't remember if it was a dream or it had happened. Most of her time back then was a total black hole where there should be memories.

Her therapist had suggested that if she wanted to remember them, she could be hypnotized. She was not desperate to dredge up those memories. They were best left buried under a cloud of darkness, but that dream with Preston had seemed so real and so passionate.

She had woken up aroused and sweaty, even though the

air conditioner was on. She had feared that she was having a relapse.

Thankfully, her body had calmed down after a cold shower. Her wits were still with her.

She should have said hi to Preston last night, but she didn't have the guts. She wondered if he had recognized her.

She slipped into the back of the conference room. There were approximately sixteen persons in the room; some faces she recognized from the head office, and some were new to her. She was hoping to go unnoticed, but Noel was just doing introductions and called her out before she could sit.

"Everybody this is Sheryl Stone, Carragon's top sales representative for two years running. Hopefully, she will repeat her sales magic here in Jamaica."

Sheryl nodded and smiled.

"And to start her off on her way to showing you all how it is done, she will be getting the tough cookie to tango with."

"Huh?" Sheryl frowned.

"While you were on your way we were discussing retail outlets, such as supermarkets, especially the ones that are not yet carrying our particular brands. It was shocking to discover that one of the biggest supermarket chains here in Jamaica is not carrying our products. They are what the local sales staff call the tough cookie."

Sheryl nodded. "Okay. Who are they?"

"Wiley Groceries." Noel looked over at her. "They have thirty-six outlets island wide. They are too much of a huge account to let slip through our fingers. First order of business, Sheryl…go get that account."

Sheryl swallowed. "Did you say Wiley Groceries?"

"Yes." Noel nodded. "Rumor has it that the head of the company had a fall out with the old management and refused to carry their merchandise. It's up to you to convince Wiley

Groceries that there is new management in town and we are very nice people."

Noel grinned when he said it, but Sheryl did not see the joke.

Wiley Groceries. She had to do her homework.

It was hard for Sheryl to concentrate during the rest of the meeting. She was shown to her office after the meeting, and she made a beeline for her computer. She needed to find out more about Wiley Groceries.

Chapter Nine

"Preston, you have a minute?" Walter poked his head around the office door.

"I am not sure," Preston said drolly. He was staring unseeingly through the window.

"Why are you so distracted?" Walter asked, coming into the room fully.

"I saw a lady last night when I went to dinner with the senior managers, a dinner which you missed by the way." Preston turned his head and looked at Walter.

"Sorry, I had other plans. My charity, Food for the Homeless, had a fundraising event. I told you."

"I know, I gave your apologies." Preston's eyes clouded over, "She was gorgeous, the woman I saw."

"And?" Walter grinned.

"And, I don't know," Preston spread his arms, "my wires are a little crossed…she looked very familiar. She felt familiar. I should have gone over and said something, but when I looked back, she had already left. I sit here now wondering if I had dreamt her up."

"Intriguing," Walter murmured. "You'll get over it."

"Thanks so much for your concern." Preston smiled lazily. "What is it that you wanted?"

"Last night, I heard from a good source that Greenland Distributors is under new management, apparently the company who took them over, got some new staff and the slate was wiped clean."

"Which means your beef with Gary Green is over?" Preston smiled. "Good. We can now carry their products."

"Shunning them was not all bad. We pushed our own brand and profited handsomely. Gary was a weasel," Walter muttered. "Refusing to carry his products was a lesson in humility for him."

"Fine." Preston shrugged. "I didn't interfere then, and I would prefer not to get into this now."

"I know." Walter nodded. "The strategy is to wait for the new owners to approach us. I don't want us to look eager in the least. Let them woo us. We are still the ones with the upper hand. "

"Okay." Preston nodded. "So I am assuming you want me to deal with this new account instead of Melissa. She will be angry, you know she likes to stick to the chain of command."

"Yes." Walter nodded. "You deal with it. After a senior managers' meeting, Melissa is usually like putty. She thinks you are the best boss in the world."

"I think I have the best senior staff in the world. You all make me look good." Preston smirked. "I will do what you bid me to, Walter Wiley. Is that all?"

"Yes." Walter moved to the door. "Oh, and one more thing. There is a night cricket match at Sabina Park. I would love to take my nephew. I have an extra VIP ticket."

"He'll be ecstatic," Preston said. "He's a sports fanatic like you and Jordan."

"I'll pick him up at six," Walter said exiting the office.

Preston looked at his schedule. He had a meeting with Catherine Preddy and her team from marketing in an hour. They had recently rolled out their own brand of Wiley snacks. It was an important meeting. He had been the one to spearhead the drive to personalize some generic snacks and turn them into Wiley branded products. He got updates from the marketing and distribution team on a quarterly basis.

They had been doing so well far, and he was thinking of adding even more products to the line.

He had to put thoughts of that woman from last night from his mind. When the phone rang, he saw that it was Helena. He almost told her to give him five minutes.

His reaction was quite unlike him, usually, nothing messed with his focus, but there was something about that woman that was scrambling his mind.

He picked up the phone. "Yes, Helena."

"Boss," Helena almost squealed in his ear. "There is a Sheryl Stone from Carragon Jamaica Ltd on the phone. She wants to speak with you."

Preston froze.

"Boss, I think it's her!" Helena was beside herself with excitement. "She is in Jamaica! She's the new senior sales rep."

"Thanks, Helena. Put her through." Preston inhaled shakily, and then it clicked. Last night—his sense of familiarity. If he had gotten the chance to see her close up, he would have known that the lady staring at him through the glass had been Sheryl.

"Hello, Preston." It was her voice all right. She had a slight accent, but it was her. "I don't know if you remember me, but we knew each other as children."

Preston couldn't sit to take the phone call. He stood up. He was nervous. He needed to get a hold of himself.

"Sheryl Stone, of course, I remember you." He cleared his throat. "What a surprise!"

"I know." Sheryl sounded nervous as well, somehow that made him relax a little. "Can we meet?"

"Why didn't you say hello last night?" Preston asked.

"You recognized me?" Sheryl asked surprise evident in her voice.

"Not really." Preston rubbed his temples, "I don't know what made me look over but I couldn't shake the encounter from my mind. I have so many questions to ask. I am feeling pretty overwhelmed here. Are you okay again? What happened between then and now? So many questions..."

Sheryl made a whimpering sound. "Preston can we not talk about the past? I just want to talk about the possibility of Wiley Groceries taking our goods."

"That's all?" Preston asked incredulously.

"Yes," Sheryl said coldly. "I came to Jamaica to work. This is my job. You are a potentially big account."

Preston couldn't believe his ears. He was stunned into silence for a long time. Why was she so hostile?

"I am sorry." She sighed down the phone. "I get defensive about my past. That's why I didn't come over to say hello. I was just planning to avoid everything and pretend it never happened. Unfortunately, you are in the past category."

"I see," Preston whispered, disbelief making him numb.

"Can we meet today?" Sheryl asked again.

"No," Preston said. "Sorry, I am busy."

"Tomorrow?" Sheryl asked.

"No," Preston grunted. "Maybe if you would call my secretary she can arrange a meeting time. She knows my schedule best."

"Are you snubbing me?" Sheryl asked incredulously.

"I would never snub Sheryl Stone, my childhood friend and a girl I knew from I was twelve," Preston said testily. "If that Sheryl had called I would clear my schedule. We could go to lunch, catch up on old times.

"I would love to find out more about what she has been up to these past couple of years. I would love to hear about Miss Pam. You guys left Portland so abruptly I would love to fill in the blanks.

"But you are not that Sheryl." Preston paused. "And I am not too eager to talk business with Carragon Jamaica Ltd at this moment. Goodbye Miss Stone."

He hung up the phone and then dropped the handset back in the cradle. He had to take a walk. He didn't want to think about what he had just done.

He just hung up on the woman he had spent all morning thinking about. At least that mystery was now solved.

Sheryl had blossomed into a beauty. The girl had grown into a gloriously fascinating looking woman, and she sounded like she had all her wits about her.

All his fears of her being in less fortunate circumstances were unfounded. He breathed a sigh of relief.

But she was obviously not interested in trading personal stories of the past. She just wanted to talk business.

What was she so afraid of?

Maybe she was afraid of him bringing up her mental health or the baby she gave up for adoption. Maybe she wasn't afraid but ashamed of it all, and that's why he was in the past category as she had put it.

What if she doesn't call back?

She would. She had revealed her hand; Wiley Groceries was a potentially big account.

He chuckled to himself and headed for the door. Oh, she would be back. Gary Green and his team had hounded him for years to carry their products. Why should this new company be any different?

Conquering a Wiley Groceries account would be the feather in any salesperson's cap. If Sheryl was ambitious, she would want to be the one to do it.

"Helena." He sat across from his assistant, who was rapidly typing something on her computer.

"One minute, boss." Helena looked at him. "I am just finishing that memo you gave me earlier to the senior staff."

Preston nodded and waited.

Helena finished her last line and then looked over at him. "So you found her?"

"She found me," Preston said. "Call off that detective, will you? I do not need him now."

"Yes, sir." Helena nodded.

"I snubbed her." Preston looked at his watch. "If she is a good saleswoman she will call back, she wants our business. After my meeting with the marketing team, I will be having lunch in the supermarket cafe. Let that slip when you refuse to put her through to me and don't schedule me for a meeting with her. Stall her."

"Intriguing." Helena smiled. "You are playing hard to get."

Preston nodded. "Yes, I am. I am going to walk the shop floor, will be back in time for my meeting. After that clear me for the rest of the day."

"Okay boss." Helena looked at him concerned. "Does she know about Pete, that you have him?"

"No." Preston got up, "and maybe she'll never know because she doesn't want to discuss the past."

****

"You lucked out with Wiley Groceries?" Noel came to her office and took one look at her shocked face and assumed the worst.

She hadn't moved since Preston hung up on her. It served her right; she had been obnoxious and insulting.

She looked up at Noel who had his arms crossed and was looking at her warmly. "You can't win them all, at least not with a simple phone call."

"I know." Sheryl nodded. "I have been doing this for years. You don't have to tell me that."

"Good." Noel nodded. "I know you are an expert that's why I gave you the tough cookie."

Sheryl nodded. "Excuse me. I am going to have to do some begging."

Noel laughed. "I will leave you to it."

Sheryl picked up the phone, inhaled deeply and then dialed Preston's office number.

"Preston Wiley's office, Helena speaking." His assistant came on the line.

"Hello again." Sheryl forced her voice to sound as pleasant as an usher on a church porch. "May I speak with Preston Wiley?"

"Who may I say is calling?" Helena asked briskly.

"Sheryl Stone from Carragon Jamaica."

"Oh," Helena paused, "Miss Stone, Mr. Wiley is not in office right now."

"He said I should ask you about scheduling me for a meeting with him." Sheryl paused. "Is a meeting possible for this week?"

"No can do," Helena said almost cheerfully. "Mr. Wiley is booked solid for the next few weeks. Maybe I can pencil you in for a date in April?"

"Goodness, that's six weeks away," Sheryl muttered. "He

is snubbing me."

"He is?" Helena asked interestedly. "I wouldn't say that he always has his stuff planned way in advance. He only makes exceptions for family and friends."

"Can I just show up?" Sheryl asked, "will he see me then?"

"Hmm," Helena sounded like she was considering it, "not at the office. He does eat lunch most days in the Yum Yum Cafe between twelve-thirty and one-thirty."

"Where is that?" Sheryl asked jotting down the name.

"At the supermarket. There is a Yum Yum in all our major outlets."

"Yes," Sheryl said sheepishly. She needed to do more homework on Wiley Groceries. Obviously, the business had grown beyond her recognition. "Thank you."

"Don't mention it," Helena said briskly. "And I mean it. Don't tell anyone that I told you this."

"Sure. Thanks again." Sheryl hung up the phone. It was just after ten. She had two hours to do her homework and then show up casually at Yum Yum.

A quick phone call to Noel and five minutes later she had Luna Townsend sitting in her office. She was the salesperson that was previously assigned to get the Wiley Groceries account.

Luna was a half Asian woman with bleached blond hair and black eyebrows that she drew in a little bit too close to each other with a black eyebrow pencil.

Sheryl forced herself to stop staring at her weird boxy eyebrows. "Tell me about Wiley Groceries she said after exchanging pleasantries with Luna."

"What do you want to know?" Luna asked.

"Everything," Sheryl said. "I need to know everything."

"I have a file," Luna said exiting the office quickly and then returning with a file folder and a magazine.

"This is the layout of the supermarket. These are the personal care products they carry from our competitors. They even have a makeup and makeover section. I have been trying to get them to take our brands but to no avail."

"I know," Sheryl said skipping through the book. "What happened?"

Luna sighed. "I have no clue, but it has something to do with our old CEO, Gary Green and Walter Wiley. Walter Wiley is the VP of Finance at Wiley Corp, a member of the board and brother to the chairman, Preston Wiley."

"Gary probably had no idea that stepping on one Wiley toe was stepping on them all. They stopped carrying our stuff two years ago. It messed with the profits and screwed up our quotas. I guess that's why Gary sold the business."

"Okay," Sheryl nodded, "I'll see what I can do to get Wiley Groceries back on our books."

"Oh, and this is a recent article which came out in Caribbean Finance Magazine about Preston Wiley."

Sheryl took it from Luna and stared at the cover.

Preston was in a suit his hands folded, a half smile on his face.

"He is a beautiful man," Luna said dreamily. "The picture does him justice, trust me. I have seen him in real life."

Sheryl nodded. "Can I borrow this?"

"I want it back," Luna said, a warning in her voice. "I already had to rescue it from other people in this office, twice."

Sheryl grinned. "Okay, ma'am."

When Luna left she eagerly skipped through the article. It was revealing. The writer, Denise Graham was very good. She eagerly consumed the article.

The Wiley brothers lost everything when they were mere boys; their guardian squandered their inheritance to nothing.

Through the years they worked together to forge a formidable empire. Losing his parents early under tragic circumstances. Preston Wiley describes his early years as busy ones. So busy in fact that he had no time for fun. He describes a time when he had to juggle university and putting Wiley Groceries back in the black. He had to act as a father to his younger brothers and had to run their fledgling supermarkets with his older siblings to bring it to what it is now. It is a remarkable story if you think about it; he did all of this without adult intervention...

Sheryl lowered the magazine after reading that, she had no idea that it had gotten so bad. They had lost it all. *What had happened to Fred?*

Good heavens. She picked up the article again. *Preston Wiley says he makes time for fun these days because he knows how important the balance of work and play is in his life. For now, he is single, but he is a family man at heart.*

Sheryl leaned back in the chair. Single. Why did that put a smile on her face?

What was wrong with the women in his social circle? She grabbed her handbag and headed to HR. She needed to claim her car and then take a trip across town to Yum Yum restaurant.

Chapter Ten

Preston knew the exact moment that Sheryl stepped into Yum Yum. The cafe style restaurant with an outside shaded patio. He had chosen the table closest to the end of the patio, and he could see inside. Sheryl had taken the bait. He smiled to himself while he admired her from afar.

Her slim figure was encased in a black pantsuit. Her hair was pulled back in a slick bun that highlighted her bone structure. She looked around for him. He pretended as if he had not seen her and looked down at his laptop. He was browsing through some quarterly sales figures from his previous meeting with the marketing team. The numbers kept running into each other as he anticipated her coming over and pretending she too hadn't seen him.

He didn't have long to wait.

"Hi, Preston."

He looked up slowly. She was even prettier close-up, and those mahogany eyes were still rare and mesmerizing. He suppressed the urge to get up, hug her, and kiss away the last twelve years.

"Hello...er..." he raised an eyebrow nonchalantly.

"Sheryl." She looked mortified at his distance and his seeming forgetfulness. "Sheryl Stone. I heard that this is a nice place to eat lunch. May I join you?"

Preston nodded. "Sure. I must warn you though that I do not do business on my lunchtime."

"I understand." Sheryl sighed. "I am sorry about the call earlier."

"You are forgiven." Preston looked down at his laptop again.

"I er, I read the Caribbean Financial article about you."

"You did?" Preston looked up. "Was it good? I haven't read it yet. Denise said she would have sent over a complimentary copy."

"It was good. I had no idea you guys had it so hard after..."

Preston leaned back in his seat and stared at her fully. He glanced at her ring finger in particular and relaxed even more.

She looked away and then back at him. "I don't remember much about that time, Preston, after the accident, I mean."

Preston nodded. "I see."

"I hate talking about it." Sheryl sighed, "It took me years to stop feeling dirty. I have no real recollection of the stuff I did and with whom."

"You were not well." It was Preston's turn to feel guilty. "How did it go after you left Portland? And where on earth is Miss Pam?"

"Well after I er..." Sheryl didn't want to look at him while she talked, she looked down at her clasped hands, "after I got pregnant my mom took me to Kingston. She took me to a psychiatrist, and I was committed to a mental hospital. I was deemed a threat to myself and others."

Sheryl grimaced. "I can't remember much of what happened. I was given mild medication because my hormones were out of whack and my brain chemicals were out of whack, and they feared that I had damaged my hypothalamus from the accident and that I would be permanently you know..."

Preston nodded. "I know."

"But I had the baby, and they put me on some mood and hormone stabilizers, and my brain healed eventually. It's a very resilient organ this brain of ours." Sheryl inhaled. "I got better enough to stop taking the million and one meds I was on. By that time, my aunt Lena had filed for us. My mom and I left Jamaica two years later.

"I got my GED in the US and then eventually went to college on Carragon's dime. My mom remarried shortly after we moved to San Francisco, to a very nice man, Raul Santiago."

Preston smiled. "Really? Miss Pam remarried?"

"Yes. They run a bed and breakfast inn, in the Napa Valley. She is happy and content and doesn't want to talk about Jamaica. I told her I was coming out here and she begged me not to."

"You wanted to come?" Preston asked gently.

"Oh no." Sheryl shook her head, "but I have to do Carragon's biddings for two more years because they did pay my college tuition. And they thought I should be out here, so here I am."

"Here you are." Preston smiled, "it's a pleasure to see you again."

"Likewise." Sheryl smiled, "I recognized you instantly last night. You are still..."

"Still what?" Preston grinned.

"Handsome." Sheryl shook her head. "I had the hugest crush on you when we were younger."

"Likewise." Preston smiled. "Trust me, it was the reason I did not resist when...And here comes Walter." He leaned back in his chair. "And Saint."

Sheryl groaned. "Do you have to tell them who I am?"

"No, I don't." Preston shrugged, "but if you are planning to do business with us, they are pretty unavoidable, especially Walter. He is the VP of Finance and my deputy. Don't worry, they don't bite. Neither are they insensitive."

Sheryl swung around and looked at the men headed toward them and then gasped. "Oh my goodness. Walter is a hunk, and Saint is...my goodness!"

Preston chuckled, but he was feeling a tad bit jealous. He was used to women looking at his brothers and exclaiming, but he had never had a stroke of jealousy until now.

Walter approached the table with a tray in hand first. "Hello brother and..."

"Sheryl Stone," Preston said impatiently. He didn't want them joining them for lunch. He wanted to find out other things about Sheryl, like was she in a relationship currently and would she like to start hanging with him.

He still liked her. It was amazing how that worked. He hasn't seen her in twelve years, but his emotions didn't care one bit. Were his feelings waiting on ice until she came back into his life?

"Sheryl Stone!" Walter's exclamation busted his little self-examination. "Hey! How are you?"

Saint came over too and greeted her as he had predicted. They were polite and showed not one lick of undue emotion. He knew that they would be at his house as soon as he got home, prodding him for details about Sheryl.

He also knew that they wouldn't intrude now. Walter took one look at his expression and then turned to smile at Sheryl. "It's nice to see you again."

"And me too," Saint said, "we are going to eat in my office. See you later, Preston."

Preston nodded. It was a loaded 'see you later'.

"They are grown now." Sheryl chuckled. "I remember them as little boys. I just never thought about how they would look as men. I especially remember Saint having a cute gap-toothed smile. Now he has perfect pearly white teeth. Walter is so much taller than I remember him being and he is obviously working out. He looks like he could bench-press me."

Preston groaned. "Walter the hunk."

Sheryl laughed her face lighting up. "How are Jordan and Case and Guy? And Shawn?"

"Jordan is away in Dubai. He'll be back for Saint's wedding in August. Case was on tour. He got back yesterday. He's a gospel artiste. You must have heard the song, God is Closer Than You Think by C. Wiley. It is pretty popular."

"Yes, I have, and I love it." Sheryl clapped her hand. "I never knew that was Case! Last time I saw him, he was a very cute curly haired boy, with an adorable little way to bat his long eyelashes."

Preston laughed. "Now he hates his eyelashes. He says they make him look girly."

Sheryl chuckled. "And Guy what happened to him?"

"Guy is a farmer. He specializes in strawberries. He is thinking of expanding into mangoes, but I have no idea when he is going to take on that project."

"He has always loved farming." Sheryl nodded. "I remember how much he used to talk about his vegetable garden."

Preston smiled. "Now he can't shut up about his farm and whatever book he is currently reading."

"Where on earth is Shawn?" Sheryl asked after a pause.

"I've always liked that girl. She was flamboyant and bold and irreverent and said what was on her mind. I hope she hasn't changed."

"Not in the least," Preston said dryly. "Shawn is still Shawn. She comes to Jamaica often, well not so much when Jordan is not here. She is an architect like Jordan."

"Are they married yet?" Sheryl asked.

"No." Preston shook his head. "They are running rings around each other like they are in a circus but now that Jordan is away, who knows?"

"And you," Preston changed the subject, "are you married?"

"No." Sheryl shook her head. "I was engaged once, but it didn't work out. Ironically, he is now my boss in Jamaica."

"Ouch, that should be awkward, I know it's a pain to work with exes."

"What about you?" Sheryl asked eagerly. "I know the article said you are single, but it didn't say if you are committed to anybody."

"No commitments only to my son at the moment." Preston watched her closely while he said that.

"You have a son?" Sheryl asked surprised.

"Yep." Immediately, Preston regretted telling her. He didn't want her asking about Pete's mother and all of that. He was not ready to tell Sheryl about Pete. Telling her about Pete was something that he had to work up to. He could imagine her paralyzed with shock if he just blurted out, "Hey, remember that son you gave up for adoption, I am his father, and I have him now."

He needed time, and he suspected that she did too. He needed to know if she was even remotely interested in children. He couldn't subject Pete to another rejection or abandonment now.

"Well," Sheryl's eyes clouded over, "good for you. You are a single dad?"

"Yes." Preston diverted the conversation before she could ask him more things he had no intention of pursuing. "What are you doing this evening?"

"I was planning to buy groceries, unpack," Sheryl shrugged, "and then take a walk over to Emancipation Park, it is pretty close to my apartment. I left before it was officially opened. I want to explore it and see if it is a reasonable alternative to a gym membership."

"Would you like some company?" Preston asked.

"For which part of it exactly?" Sheryl squinted at him.

"All of it." Preston grinned. "I am good at grocery shopping and walking in the park."

"I thought you were booked until April?" Sheryl asked him. "How could you have all of this spare time to spend with little old me?"

"I canceled the rest of the meetings I had today," Preston smiled, "when I told Helena to send you here."

"Are you serious?" Sheryl grinned, "I was set up."

"I wouldn't call it set up." Preston murmured. "I was hoping that Sheryl Stone, the girl from my childhood, would show up so we could talk."

"So when can Sheryl Stone, salesperson, speak to you?" Sheryl asked.

"I don't know yet. I'll let you know. Are you going to eat lunch? After that, we can go shopping. I know of a supermarket where you can get the best stuff."

Sheryl laughed.

****

She had spent six solid hours with Preston Wiley.

Sheryl sat on her bed after leaving the shower; she was just too keyed up to sleep. Today was going to play over and over in her head like a broken record. She was going to analyze every last bit of it and wasn't going to stop smiling.

She was happy that nobody could see her now as she sprawled out on the bed with her towel wrapped snuggly around her, staring up at the ceiling, and grinning like a Cheshire cat.

He was perfect. Personality wise, Preston was still the boy she had liked back in their younger years. He still had that relatable sense of humor. He was still caring and considerate. By the time they had finished shopping for groceries, and they had come to her apartment she had felt relaxed in his company, even though he had insisted on paying for the groceries.

She was relaxed but aware of him as a very desirable male. He treated her with the kind of easy camaraderie that made her let down her guard, which was a lethal combination. She had probably gone a little overboard and did a little bit too much sharing.

He had looked at the black and white living room and asked her if she still liked the color turquoise.

She was shocked that he remembered. Of course, she still liked turquoise, but it wasn't her favorite color currently. She was more into yellow these days—bright unashamed bold sunshiny yellows. She had then had gone on to tell him about the yellow accent wall in her Nob Hill basement apartment.

He had quizzed her about her life in San Francisco, and she had not shut up about it. She had told him about her Aunt Lena and how bohemian she was and that she ran an art gallery in downtown San Francisco and how she had several kooky art friends, who she was constantly introducing to Sheryl.

And when they were walking in the park, which had some

decent walking trails but nothing as strenuous as she was used to, he had suggested that they try something a bit more challenging by going walking up to Widcombe Heights in the mornings. It was a stretch of road that ended at the top of a mountain that had breathtaking views of Kingston.

"It's close to where I live." Preston had offered the information casually. "You can park your car at my complex, and we could go walking from there. I guarantee you; you will not think it's tame."

She had said yes. Of course, she had. She wanted to spend more time with him. She was hooked.

Besides, she wanted to learn more about Preston. Today they focused mostly on her, but she wanted to know about him. She wanted to know about his son and the boy's mother and if Preston still had feelings for her.

How often did he see him? Did the boy live with his mother?

She had always thought that Preston would be the first to get married and start a family. Being a single father was the last thing she expected of him.

She wasn't judging, but maybe there was a little flaw in his perfect persona? Perhaps he was terrible in relationships.

She turned over on her belly and closed her eyes. She hoped she didn't have that erotic dream about the two of them again tonight. She needed her beauty rest to get up at five o'clock to go walking with him.

Chapter Eleven

Another night. Another family meeting. Preston looked at his brothers as he came down the stairs. He headed to the living room, and they followed.

He had just told Pete goodnight. The poor boy was so hyped by his first live cricket match that he doubted that he would sleep but as soon as his head hit the pillow, he was out.

"Your life is becoming rather interesting." Case was the first to speak. "I go away for two months and return to find I have a nephew…"

"If you go away again when you return he will have a wife." Saint chuckled. You should have seen him with Sheryl today; he was looking at her as if he had just won a prize.

"And he didn't want us to talk to her," Walter murmured. "He gave me the look. The go away look. We could barely say hello before he was shooing us away with his eyes."

"How did she look?" Guy asked.

"Good," Walter said, "very good. She is a beautiful woman. Update us, Preston. We are curious. How did Sheryl suddenly appear in your life?"

Preston told them. They silently listened.

Saint was the one who asked. "So she doesn't know that Pete is the son she gave up for adoption?"

"No," Preston responded. "And you will all shut up about it. I will tell her in my own time when I think she is ready to hear."

"So you are going to be seeing her," Guy asked, "as in dating her?"

"I want us to get to know each other again," Preston said. "I wouldn't call it dating. I'd call it friendship."

"Okay." Walter wrinkled his brow. "We will play along with this friendship idea."

"I am serious," Preston said. "I want us to be friends."

Guy yawned. "Well, I am looking forward to seeing her again; bring her to the farm on Sunday. Take Pete too. You can make it a family outing."

"That's not a bad idea," Preston said, "but I am not going to jump into introducing her to my son and having them spend loads of time together."

"How is the adoption process going?" Walter asked. "Pete has been introducing himself as Peter Wiley all evening. That boy desperately wants to use his right surname."

"I know." Preston nodded, "he has been saying he is Peter Wiley since his second day here. I signed the papers and sent them off to the Committee. Jaylee checks in on us every two weeks. Last week she only called. She wanted me to invite her to dinner. I told her that Pete and I were eating out."

Walter laughed. "She is seriously messed up if she thinks that browbeating you into dating her will get her anywhere."

"Seriously," Preston muttered, "I didn't know she was like

this.”

“So you had a lucky escape,” Guy said. “Give God thanks and praises for that. I am going to bounce; I have a full day ahead of me tomorrow.”

“Me too,” Saint said standing up and stretching. “You should invite Sheryl to the wedding as your plus one.”

Walter got up as well, “better yet invite her to church. I am having a potluck at my place this Sabbath. We can all get to say hello then.”

“Okay.” Preston nodded, “I don’t know if she will want to come. She is skittish about her past and meeting people from it.”

“Tell her we don’t bite,” Walter said heading to the door with his other brothers. “Besides it’s us. Assure her that we are nonjudgmental people. She has already said hi, anyway.”

“Aren’t you going too?” Preston looked at Case.

“I don’t think so,” Case shook his head, “I’ll crash in your guest room.”

“You have a whole house for yourself.” Preston chuckled.

“I know,” Case said sleepily, “but I can’t be bothered to go over there. Night.”

“Night.” Preston smiled to himself as Case headed upstairs.

“By the way, I am going walking with Sheryl tomorrow morning at five. I’ll be back at six, six-thirty.”

“Have fun,” Case said, “I could make breakfast if you want.”

“No.” Preston shook his head, “As a matter of fact; I would love if you were not up, just in case she comes over.”

“Okay, got you,” Case said. “What time does Pete wake up?”

“Seven.”

“Well, then I won’t be up until seven.” Case chuckled. “I’ll make breakfast then, or better yet, you make it. I have my mind on pancakes the way you do it."

Preston smiled. "Fine, welcome home little brother."

"As usual, I'm glad to be here." Case gave him a salute and headed to his usual room.

****

"I thought you said you were fit." Preston laughed at Sheryl as she struggled to put one foot before the other on their way up Widcombe Heights. A cock crowed in the distance, and he could hear Sheryl's tortured gasps for air as they steadily walked up the elevated road. Quite a few early morning walkers were out even though the air was nippy and it was barely light out. The trees at the side of the road were dripping with morning dew.

"Walking on a treadmill and walking on these streets are not the same." Sheryl finally admitted. "Goodness!"

Preston grinned. "I used to do this with Case and Saint every morning, except we ran it twice."

"Show off." Sheryl stopped and inhaled raggedly. "This hill is probably sloping at 45 degrees in some places. My legs feel like noodles."

"You'll get used to it." Preston pointed at an older couple that had passed them and were mere dots in the distance. "They obviously did."

"I don't think I'll be here that long." Sheryl snorted. "I am just here for two years."

"That's a long time for you to make up your mind." Preston winked at her. "You may just want to stay."

"I don't know." Sheryl walked a few steps and then stopped. "We'll see."

Preston stopped and waited for her. "We have a gym at our townhouse complex if you want to work out with weights."

He didn't know why he was offering; maybe because he

looked at her in her black tracksuit and hoodie and makeup bare face and wanted to see more of her just like this every morning.

It didn't take much for him to get fanciful where Sheryl was concerned, did it?

"I wouldn't want to intrude; I don't want your neighbors to get the wrong idea." Sheryl inhaled and looked around.

"My neighbors are my brothers," Preston said. "We are the only ones living in the townhouses. And only one of the six of us uses the gym religiously."

"Walter." Sheryl grinned. "I can see that. How did you all manage to live together like that?"

"Shawn designed it, and Jordan oversaw the project," Preston said. "We got the land as part of a package for the commercial property. Jordan thought it was a good thing to have us living in the same community. We are like the Wiley tribe. We just live in different huts."

Sheryl giggled. "Those houses are the most sophisticated huts I have ever seen."

"Shawn and Jordan work well together." Preston folded his arms. "You are going to walk or what?"

"I am busted," Sheryl pulled the hoodie over her head, "and I am a bit tired. I didn't get much sleep last night."

"Okay, we'll go to the top and take in the view another morning, the sunrise is simply spectacular. The air is fresh, the place is still, and the golden light comes over and bathes the town. Kingston looks pretty from up there. It looks like a young fresh town with limitless possibilities for the day."

"You make it sound so good." Sheryl inhaled, "but I know my limits."

Preston looked at her. "You should have tried to stay in and get some extra shuteye if you didn't get much sleep."

"It wouldn't have made a difference." Sheryl stopped and

stretched. "It's good to get out in the fresh air. I am trying to escape my dreams, staying in bed would be torture."

"What kind of dreams are you having?" Preston asked the question innocently, but then Sheryl started acting weird.

She looked away from him guiltily. "I'd prefer not to say."

"Oh, those kinds of dreams." Preston chuckled. "Who are the stars in your dreams?"

Sheryl stopped and looked at him. "You and me."

Preston pushed his hand into his tracksuit pocket and froze when Sheryl candidly admitted that. A group of people walked around them, and all he could do was gawp at her.

She held his gaze in the charged silence only speaking when the group was out of earshot. "I shouldn't have admitted that. I am sorry."

"It's okay." Preston looked at her quizzically. "Describe the dream."

"Hell no." Sheryl shook her head. "I can't."

"Did we have clothes on?" Preston asked.

"Preston!" Sheryl looked at him aghast. "I will not discuss this further. Drop it."

"I am sorry," Preston said no hint of repentance in his voice. "It's nice to know you dream about me."

"No, it's not." Sheryl inhaled. "I have been celibate since my whole mental breakdown. Now I am having these dreams. They feel so real. I almost thought I was having a relapse."

"Are you?" Preston asked concerned.

"No." Sheryl sniffed. "I am in my right mind, but those dreams are highly charged. I only started having them after seeing you at the restaurant. Maybe I shouldn't see you anymore."

"Or maybe you should see more of me," Preston countered, "and they will disappear."

Sheryl grimaced. "Probably. I doubt it though. I'll test

the theory, but if they keep happening, I am going to start avoiding you."

Preston grinned. "No, you will not. You like getting to know me again; I can see it on you. I like getting to know you again too so don't think this is one-sided. For instance, I just learned that you've been celibate; I like the sound of that."

"Such double standards. You haven't been. You have a child with a woman, and you are not married!" Sheryl glanced at him angrily. "Was your relationship with her serious?"

She is jealous! Preston stared at her for long moments trying to formulate what to tell her about his son's mother.

"Well, we weren't in a committed relationship when he was conceived." Preston answered carefully, "we...er...our coming together was not planned."

"What's your relationship with her like?" Sheryl couldn't keep the resentment from her voice.

"We are civil," Preston said carefully. "It's a very long story. I'd like to tell you about it one day, but not today."

"I am acting crazy." Sheryl stopped. "I came into your life yesterday, and I am..."

"Jealous," Preston said, "about every relationship that I have ever had because deep down you want to think of me as being yours exclusively."

"Something like that," Sheryl said sheepishly. "You are incredibly perceptive."

"Not really, I feel the same about you," Preston said, "but I don't hold your past against you. I know you weren't in your right mind. I just don't like thinking about the relationships you had when you were in your right mind. Does that make sense?"

"Yes, somehow it does." Sheryl nodded. "I had one serious relationship. That's it, one. And I decided to tell him about my past. I told him I was mentally ill for a while and that I had a baby that I gave away and he dumped me the same night."

"I vowed never to talk about my past with anyone again, but here you are. You already know my past."

Preston tugged her hoodie closer to her head. "Therefore no need to hide."

"No need to hide," Sheryl repeated. "It feels good."

"You want to talk about that baby you gave up for adoption?" Preston asked when they walked in companionable silence for a while.

"Nope." Sheryl looked at him. "Not today. I am not sure I ever will be ready."

"When you are ready to talk, I am here." Preston looked around. It was getting light out as they neared the townhouse complex.

Shawn had named it The Wiley's. He could see the black letters on the cream-colored stucco wall.

"Have lunch with me today," Preston said before they reached the gates.

"I came here to work, you know." Sheryl sniffed. "I am not exactly on vacation."

"Oh, that's right." Preston grinned. "We'll have a business lunch."

"As in, we can seriously talk about your supermarkets carrying Carragon products?" Sheryl frowned. "Or are we still not talking about that?"

"Might as well get it out of the way," Preston grinned at her, "so that you can't make excuses to yourself like, I have to be friendly to Preston Wiley because he is a prospective client."

"That was your plan wasn't it?" Sheryl glared at him. "Lead me along because you know I want this."

"Yes," Preston said, no hint of shame in his voice, "but I don't want your attention or time because you want my business. I want it out of the way. So lunchtime we get it out of the way.

Sheryl smiled. "Good. Thank you."

"And if you stop taking my calls or show up to exercise after you have my business, I'll just think you are a user." Preston continued, "a sick user."

Sheryl chuckled. "Is that so?"

"And if you don't come to church with me on Sabbath I'll think even worst things about you."

Sheryl laughed. "You can give me directions at lunch today. I was thinking of joining a church family while here anyway. I was just not sure where to go. My mom's old church had turned their backs on us when they heard that I was an unmarried pregnant girl. They were even insisting that my mom had me do some exorcism. She had refused to do so. Obviously, she was not convinced that it would work. My mom had stopped going to church all together. She only started going back with Raul a couple of years ago."

"So that's where Miss Pam got it from." Preston whistled. "I remember she was pretty much against a psychiatrist after your accident and you er… stripped in the kitchen for me."

"Shut up." Sheryl pointed at him. "I wasn't in my right mind I can't even remember that. It's not nice to make fun of mentally ill people."

"A formerly mentally ill person." Preston smiled. "I am sorry. I wasn't making fun of you. It's just that…that moment was indelibly printed on my mind."

He reached the gate and opened it. "I was fifteen years old, and that was my first time seeing breasts live. I just sat there while you stripped, contemplating how fortunate I was. Pastor Tate caught me with my mouth opened sitting paralyzed around the table, and your mother dragged you from the kitchen stark naked."

Sheryl frowned. "You see why I don't want to talk about my past?"

"Yes," Preston shrugged, "but to my knowledge, you never stripped for any of my brothers. So you can be comfortable around them if you see them."

"But they know about me." Sheryl frowned, "I hate that."

"They are decent guys, all of them," Preston said, "and trust me when I say, not one of us have foot in mouth disease. They won't bring it up if you don't."

"By the way, you'll see most of them at church if you come by. Walter is an elder, Case directs the choir, Guy spends most of his time in the sound room, and Saint plays the organ or the piano, whichever they want him to. Please don't let the fact that they'll be there stop you from coming."

"Okay," Sheryl said doubtfully. "Your brothers all do something? What do you do at church?"

"They have me teaching the preteen class, the ten to twelve-year-olds." Preston grinned, "They call me Uncle Preston."

Sheryl laughed. "Really?"

"Yes." Preston nodded. "It's quite fun."

Sheryl reached her car door and disarmed it. "You are almost too good to be true."

"What do you mean?" Preston frowned.

"You check all the boxes," Sheryl said cryptically. "See you at lunch."

She got in the car and drove away leaving him smiling. He didn't move from where he was standing for a full minute.

Chapter Twelve

"**I** can't believe you did it." Noel looked at her, a comical look of surprise on his face when she walked into the office that evening.

"I did though," Sheryl smiled, "I made my quota for two quarters."

"Just like that." Noel looked down at the invoice and then at her. "You are as amazing as Maci said."

"That's right." Sheryl grinned. But in this case, she had only needed to show up.

She had a prolonged lunch with Preston, and he had been remarkably professional. There was no banter and no teasing. He had taken her product suggestions, made some recommendations of his own and then ushered her out of his office to attend another meeting. He had hastily said that he would call.

Preston was utterly business-like. It was a sight to behold. The man knew his business inside and out. He knew products and how well they would sell, and he knew comparative prices and how best to position specific products. He was a genius retail man.

He had done his homework on Carragon products. Besides, he had previous data from their business with Greenwood. Data that he brought to mind quickly and easily.

"Who did you speak with?" Noel asked her suspiciously. She had zoned him out.

"Preston Wiley, the CEO," Sheryl raised an eyebrow, "why?"

"This guy?" Noel picked up the magazine from the top of the folder that Luna had given to her.

"Yes." Sheryl nodded.

"He was the one at the restaurant?" Noel narrowed his eyes and closed the office door. "Sheryl, I am not one to question how my sales reps do their business once it is above board and reputable."

"What are you implying?" Sheryl snapped.

"I am not implying anything." Noel growled, "but you did in a day what others sales reps tried for years and couldn't accomplish. You, Sheryl who..."

"What?" Sheryl narrowed her gaze at him. "Say it, and I'll walk. Say what you are thinking, and I will take my bag and walk out of here into the sunset, and I won't come back because this is not a conversation fit for business.

"You are paranoid; I knew that telling you anything would be dangerous. What do you think I did, walk into his office, strip, had sex with him and magically got him to do my bidding?"

"I don't know," Noel sighed, "you are an attractive woman, you used to do it in the past."

"I had a brain injury, and my reasoning was impaired. How many times am I going to have to tell you this?"

"I am sorry," Noel said stubbornly, "but something is fishy here."

"You got the Wiley Groceries business, be satisfied with that and leave me alone."

"Something is going on between you two," Noel said. "I saw the way you looked at him in the restaurant, you knew him before…"

"And?" Sheryl growled.

"And it's obvious that your sales techniques are suspect," Noel glared at her, "and that you are not the woman that I thought you were."

"I am tired of this." Sheryl stood up and got her things together. "I am going home. You are a jealous cow that could not handle the news of my past, and you obviously cannot work with me. Every time you open your big mouth, it's an insult."

"You are right. I am jealous." Noel pushed his hands into his pockets. "I am sorry if I am wrong and you didn't use your previous association and obviously womanly charm on this Preston guy. We never went further than a kiss when we were together. I assumed that you were preserving yourself for marriage..."

Sheryl sighed. "We are a long way past this discussion. This was more than a year and a fiancé ago. You moved on, washed your hands of me. You have no right to be talking to me about this now…especially at work. You are out of order. I am going home to have a hot shower and get some sleep. You need to get yourself together, boss."

She sneered the last bit in his face and then pushed past him and was out the door. "See you Monday. I hope you'll have it together by then."

Noel looked at her skeptically. "What are you doing this weekend?"

"None of your beeswax," Sheryl said through gritted teeth. "However, if you must know, there will be no prostitution involved. I will more likely be in church than on the side streets."

Luna was passing by and stopped. "You are not leaving with my magazine are you?"

"No," Sheryl handed it to her, "you can have it back."

"Thanks." Luna looked between her and Noel.

"What sort of conversation are you two having, I heard prostitution and I heard church can I eavesdrop?"

"No." Sheryl glared at Noel. "Have a nice weekend, Luna."

Eat dirt, Noel! She resisted the urge to say that out loud. She was angry enough to have said it, but she had long since learned how to control her impulses.

She went downstairs, got in her car, started it, and then turned on the radio. She searched until she found a gospel station. Take Me To The King, by Tamela Mann came on. It was a new song, and she paused for a long time listening to the lyrics. By the time it was finished, she felt calmer.

She smiled to herself. That is why gospel songs were her favorite. They had the power to lift her from zero to a hundred in a minute.

She heaved a sigh. It had been a mistake to tell Noel anything. She was going to be very sure and extremely secure with Preston before she told him more of her deeper held thoughts—her son for instance.

He had casually asked her to tell him about that time in her life but she wouldn't. She had to be absolutely sure that he could be trusted with her innermost thoughts.

For instance, she couldn't tell him that she was suffering from a deep-seated yearning to find her child, or that last night, for the first time in twelve years since his birth, she had remembered a little bit of it and that she dearly wished she could have held him a little while before they had taken him away.

She had not cared who his father was at the time. She had just cared that he was a part of her and she loved him already. In her mixed up crazy hormone-muddled-mind, she had loved him.

It was her secret, and she wasn't going to share that with anyone, not even Preston, even though he knew much of her past and didn't judge her for it.

She reached home in record time because she was driving against the traffic. She let herself into the apartment just as her cell phone began to ring. It was her mom. She reclined in her settee and answered.

"Hi, Mom."

"So you are still alive?" Her mother sniffed. "You couldn't give me a call to let me know that you arrived safely?"

"I arrived safely and started working," Sheryl said. "Today was just another regular working day."

"Can't be, Noel is your boss out there. You two were engaged; I imagine sparks are flying right about now."

"Not the way you would think." Sheryl sighed. "He is an insufferable, judgmental, intolerant...shall I go on?"

"No," her mother sighed, "it's a pity he couldn't get past the mental thing, he was perfect for you."

"No, he was not perfect," Sheryl grunted and then she thought of Preston. He was perfect for her. He was smart, intelligent, witty, and responsible. He knew everything about her and still liked her. She wondered if she should mention him to her mother.

"Guess who was my first account?" Sheryl asked after her mother brought her up to date on her and Raul and their guesthouse and Raul's grandkids who lived with him.

"The Wileys?" her mother said cautiously.

"Good guess." Sheryl murmured. "They are doing very well."

"I figured they would." Her mother sighed. "They were willing to work together and look out for each other. With the kind of determination that Jordan and Preston had, I had no doubts they would do well. I never fretted about them doing well. Tell them all a big hello from me. I have to run now. I have a frowning customer. I gotta turn that into a smile."

"Okay, Mom." Sheryl smiled and hung up the phone.

****

Preston got home later than usual that evening. It was evident that Miss Blossom had recently cleaned the place. It was gleaming and smelled perfumy.

He had asked Case to stay with Pete until he got home after Miss Blossom left. He found them in the living room watching a gospel concert. Both of them were dressed in identical jeans and white t-shirt.

Case was nodding his head to the song being played, and Pete was rocking to the music.

This kind of thing was what Case was interested in. He watched or listened to gospel music or people playing instruments.

That was the only way to entertain his youngest brother. It was a blessing. Case had been the easiest teenager to have around while they were growing up.

Pete seemed to be enjoying the video. He was singing along with the person on the screen. He had a very good singing voice. It was enough for Preston to pause before alerting them of his presence.

"Hey," Preston said to them.

"Hey." Case waved from the folds of the settee where he was sprawled out.

"Hi, dad." Pete grinned at him, "I went with Case to the studio today. I think I want to be a singer."

"He sounds good, too," Case said. "He completely blew me away. I think that particular talent skipped you and landed squarely on Pete's shoulders."

Preston laughed. "I can sing a little."

Case chuckled. "You are right. You did get a little drop of talent, but your boy is amazing. I am using him on the choir tomorrow, and with your permission, we have an appointment at a wedding in the afternoon. It's at Strawberry Hills. He will be well taken care of. Trust me, I won't let him out of my sight."

"I don't know." Preston frowned.

"Daddy, please say yes." Pete's animated face lit up. "Singing with Case was awesome. I want to be a singer when I grow up."

"Awesome, huh? So you no longer want to be a cricketer then?" Preston asked sitting across from him.

"I don't know." Pete frowned. "Can't I be both?"

"You sure can." Preston nodded, "of course both pursuits take dedication, and a fair amount of attention has to be spent perfecting each."

"I know," Pete smiled. "I can be a cricketer when I am a teenager, a singer when I am in my twenties and then run the supermarket when I am in my thirties."

Preston chuckled. "Sounds like a plan. Wiley Groceries could do with a singing cricketer at the helm."

"Case, I hope you know that you will be missing potluck at Walter's tomorrow. My friend Sheryl says she will be there. I wanted them to meet."

"Oh snap." Case glanced at Pete. "So the date is off then?"

Pete turned beseeching eyes to Preston. "Can I just say hello at church?"

Preston thought about it. A brief introduction without too many questions would be perfect. He wanted Sheryl to get to know Pete at a slow pace. Hopefully, she would get to know him without any pressure and then he'd tell her that he was her son. It was a sound and simple enough plan.

He nodded. "Yes, you can. I'll introduce her to you at church before you leave with Case."

"Who is she?" Pete asked.

"A friend from a long time ago," Preston said casually. "I liked her then, and I like her now."

Pete frowned. "Does that mean you will marry her?"

"One step at a time." Preston chuckled." And I won't marry her without your stamp of approval."

Chapter Thirteen

Preston's church was not hard to find. Sheryl arrived earlier than she would have had she been back home in San Francisco. She had slept like a log the night before; there were no dreams. She doubted that she would have moved if there had been a fire.

She had woken up refreshed and had found herself singing in the shower. She hadn't done that in a while.

She had felt so sunshiny and light that she had donned a yellow sheath dress and paired it with yellow and black heels.

She pulled back her hair and allowed it to hang free in a ponytail. She applied minimal makeup, swiped on some lip-gloss and was on her way out of the apartment in good time so traffic wouldn't cause her to be late.

She didn't encounter much, not at that time of the morning. She parked in a shaded area and strolled onto the church patio.

She was duly greeted and then ushered into the inner sanctum of the simply decorated church. The church had quite a few windows, and the breeze passed through the church in a refreshing way. She looked around for Preston, but he had told her that he didn't join the main congregation until after he was done teaching his preteen class.

They had a vibrant song service with a praise team that could rival a professional singing group. She was so into the lively song service that she missed them when they left the podium.

That used to be her and her friends, Amelia and Deborah. A wisp of nostalgia descended on her, and she could barely shake it. Her life had been filled with so much promise, but one accident had changed her course.

She had long since stopped asking God why me and started trusting him that he knew the beginning from the end. She wasn't doing all that bad these days in the trusting department, but she had lapses.

She made a valiant effort to shake the unsettling thoughts that had encroached on her good day and concentrated on the service.

She didn't know what made her look to her right, maybe because she thought she spotted Preston. But it wasn't him. It was a mini version of him. A little boy, who was probably ten or so years old. She blinked thinking her mind was playing tricks on her but he still stood at the side of the building with a group of young people. She found herself craning her neck to see him.

So that was Preston's son, had to be. The boy held himself the same way Preston did; he had the same smile, the same everything really. She had somehow thought he would have been younger maybe five or so years old.

She was still trying to process his existence as an older

child than she had thought when Preston slid into the seat beside her.

"Hello Sunshine," he smiled at her. He smelled good. *CK for men.* She remembered that scent from way back when he was a teenager. And he looked good as well. He was dressed in a charcoal gray suit and red striped tie.

She looked at his handsome face and then smiled.

"Hello, Mr. Wiley."

"Mr. Wiley?" Preston grimaced. "What did I do?"

"Nothing." Sheryl turned her head to see his son again; the boy was almost as fascinating as the man.

He was given a choir robe in a deep burgundy color by an older choir member, and someone else made sure that it fit him correctly and then they stood back and smiled with him. One of them took a picture.

"Your son is in the choir?" She turned back to Preston.

"A recent development." Preston looked at her, "You recognized him from the group of youngsters?"

"Of course, he is a mini you." Sheryl nodded. "A very handsome little fellow."

"Thank you." Preston looked at her. "I'll introduce you to him later. He is not going to be at the potluck. Case is taking him to sing at a wedding later."

"I knew that the tall curly-haired guy looked familiar." Sheryl grinned and looked back in their direction, but the choir was filing inside.

She shamelessly sought out Pete. He was at the very front, and she stared at him until he looked in her direction. She hastily looked away.

Why was she so taken up with this little boy? Maybe because he was simply adorable. He performed a solo in the first choir song and she sat and listened and joined the rest of the church in a prolonged amen. She even clapped.

She glanced at Preston her eyes shining. "He can sing! You should have captured this on tape."

Preston was observing her closely. Maybe he was wondering if she would like Pete. She saw the curiosity at the back of his eyes. Maybe he thought that she didn't like children because she gave away her own. He wasn't sure.

"Yes, he can." Preston nodded, "and it's being captured on video. Guy is in the control room under strict instructions to record everything."

"You must be so proud of him," Sheryl murmured, her voice husky. "What's his name again?"

"I am very proud of him." Preston nodded. "His name is Peter, but he likes to be called Pete."

"I like that name." Sheryl looked at Pete again. He sat in the front of the choir, so solemn and attentive. She had the insane urge to get up and hug him. She was feeling broodier than she thought or was it that she was drawn to this particular boy?

The sermon was not very good. The speaker had confessed that he wasn't good at public speaking, and he wasn't, but he got the message across. She had taken the attitude that even the most boring sermons contained a kernel of truth.

And then the service was over.

She joined Preston on the outside after they were ushered out. She was then brought face to face with Pete. He was in high demand after his performance, but Preston pulled him over.

"Pete this is my friend, Sheryl."

And he placed his hand on hers, and she found that she didn't want to let them go.

"Hello, Pete."

"Hello." He smiled at her and then the three of them stood awkwardly for a minute because she had no idea what to say to him after that. Preston didn't help matters. He was looking between the two of them in anticipation.

She felt as if she was under some kind of test. She cleared her throat. "I...er...I am going now, Preston."

"No wait," Preston said breaking the silence. "I was under the impression that you would come with me to lunch over at Walter's."

Sheryl shook her head. She just wanted to go home and weep. Something about today had her feeling emotional. Was it the fact that she was feeling a teensy weensy bit jealous of Preston and his son?

She wasn't sure what was more depressing, the thought that he had a child with someone else, or the fact that she wished he had Pete with her or the fact that she had never before been so drawn to a child. All her motherly instincts came rising to the surface when she saw Pete.

She had never felt that way about any child before.

It was this country and her memories, and she was probably hormonal, it was near that time of the month anyway.

All of it was depressing. She needed to go to the apartment and examine herself, not laugh and chat with people and keep up an appearance of lightheartedness.

"Can I take a rain check?" She looked at Preston somewhere near his shirt collar, avoiding his eyes. She then turned to Pete and looked him over. She still hadn't lost the compulsive need to hug him close. She looked him in the eyes and had to force herself to drag them away from him.

His eyes felt so familiar. So mesmeric as if they had a connection.

She needed her head examined. She was being fanciful.

"It was very nice to meet you, Pete." She croaked. Her voice was husky and tear-drenched.

Pete looked at her quizzically, but he just nodded and

smiled. He probably thought she was a weird woman.

"It was nice to meet you too, Aunty Sheryl."

Aunty Sheryl.

He called her Aunty Sheryl.

Sheryl turned and headed for her car.

Preston did not attempt to argue or stop her. And she was grateful for that because for some reason tears were gathering at the side of her eyes, and she knew she needed to release them after she did, she would feel better.

****

Preston did not call her all week, and she was partially glad about it. She needed the space. She had no reason to feel the way she did but meeting Pete had disturbed her greatly. She didn't need a psychiatrist to tell her that she was projecting her feelings of giving away her own son into this scenario and she was suffering from pangs of jealousy, pure, undiluted jealousy.

Eventually, it faded, and she started missing Preston. She had not been back in his life for that long, her missing him was puzzling.

She went to Yum Yum for lunch on the off chance that she would see him. A phone call would be too awkward after she had avoided him all week.

He wasn't on the patio where they had sat last. It was twelve-thirty though so she could be early. She ordered a small baked chicken and salad with a side of candied sweet potato and sat down at the table where she had seen Preston the last time they met at Yum Yum to eat.

She had her iPad with her, and Yum Yum offered free Wifi. She decided to catch up on her emails. She was so absorbed that she didn't hear that someone sat across from her until they cleared their throat.

She jumped and looked up. It was Walter.

He put down his tray. "May I join you?"

"Sure." Sheryl smiled at him brightly. "How are you, Walter?"

"Good." Walter smiled, "and you?"

"The same." Sheryl smiled back and then nodded to his tray. "The food here is good."

"It has to be. The boss eats here. It's an incentive for them to be consistent with the quality." Walter said grinning. "He won't be here today though. He left for Cayman on Sunday. We have a business venture on that island."

That is why she hadn't heard from him, and she had thought that Preston was mad at her because she had turned him down for the potluck.

"So when is he coming back?" Sheryl asked casually as if she didn't care.

Walter saw through her little stunt and smiled. "Tomorrow."

"So does Pete live with Preston or with his mom?" Sheryl found herself asking. Mainly because she had wondered about that all week.

"With Preston," Walter said. "Preston told me that you liked hearing Pete sing at church."

"Oh, I did." Sheryl nodded. "He has a nice vocal range."

"You like him?" Walter observed, looking at her knowingly.

"Which one?" Sheryl tried to avoid his stare.

"Both of them. Preston and Pete." Walter chuckled. "But in different ways of course."

Sheryl smirked. "Am I that obvious?"

"Not really." Walter shrugged. "It's good that you like Pete. He and Preston are a package."

"What happened in his relationship with Pete's mother?" Sheryl asked she was dying to know.

"I can't tell you sensitive information like that." Walter

started eating. "Maybe you should ask Preston. He is the best person to ask."

"You are right." Sheryl grimaced. "I am just nosy."

"What I can tell you is what happened to Gary Green and me and why we stopped doing business with him."

"Oh." Sheryl leaned forward. "I have been curious as to what caused the rift."

Walter shrugged. "We were friends. Went to the same university. His father owned the business, and then he took over. He showed a tape he had of my college girlfriend and me in a compromising position to some colleagues of mine. I don't know what his objectives were at the time, but I was royally pissed."

"You made a sex tape?" Sheryl widened her eyes.

"Technically it wasn't a sex tape, and the girlfriend was the one who filmed it." Walter winced. "It almost cost me my place at university. I think Gary, who so happened to have one of two copies, showed it to discredit me in the business community. I pulled his products from our shelves. He gave me the tape, claimed he hadn't made seconds, and begged me to do business with him again. I didn't."

Sheryl looked at him in sympathy. "I understand now."

"Yup." Walter pointed his fork at her. "You and I have a couple of things in common.

We both made some mistakes. In your case, you were mentally out of it, in my case I had no excuses. I just wanted to be different. I wanted to be young and carefree. I had never experienced the whole untroubled, light-hearted teenage feeling. My brothers and I were working hard ever since I could remember. So I got wholeheartedly into the college life. I was away from home and my older brothers and giddy with freedom. I thought I could do anything, and I did."

"But a certain kind of lifestyle has certain consequences,"

Sheryl murmured.

Walter nodded. "Yes, it does. Do you want to attend a surprise party?"

Sheryl blinked at him. "Huh. We move from talking about the past and consequences to a surprise party without a pause?"

"Sorry, I thought we were kindred spirits now. "

Sheryl laughed. "Okay Kindred Spirit, whose party are you inviting me to?"

"Guy's birthday is on Thursday. It's by the poolside at our townhouse complex. Be there by seven. He thinks we are having a simple dinner; he'll be very surprised when he sees a crowd."

Sheryl chuckled. "Okay, I'll be there."

"Good." Walter smiled at her. "Guy won't be the only one surprised if you show up."

Chapter Fourteen

Preston was sitting at the table closest to the very end of the pool area catching up with Pete on his five-day of shenanigans with his uncles. They had each put forth their best effort to entertain him and now his poor son was like an excited puppy.

Guy had brought him to his farm for two days, and he was almost giddy from the experience. He wanted to be a farmer now.

Preston's phone rang in the middle of a description about the greenhouse and the various strawberry varieties.

It was Jaylee.

"You've been avoiding me, Preston," Jaylee said her voice clipped. "May I remind you that I am necessary to your adoption process and if you refuse to take my calls I will recommend that Peter is removed from your care."

Preston sighed. "I was off the island."

Jaylee gasped dramatically. "You left Pete unsupervised,

didn't you?"

"Why would you assume that?" Preston asked willing himself not to raise his voice.

"Do you think you can manage him on your own, Preston?" Jaylee asked with faux concern. "Not because he is yours biologically means that he should necessarily stay with you."

Preston sighed. "Jaylee we've done this song and dance before. Get to the point of the call."

"How dare you?" Jaylee screeched, "I am coming over to ensure that Peter is safe and taken care of and that you are not neglecting him. I thought I could trust you without doing the bi-monthly checks, but it seems as if I can't."

"We are not at home," Preston said patiently, not rising to the bait. Jaylee wanted him to argue and then she would say he had a dreadful temper.

"Where are you?" Jaylee asked. "If I do not see the child this evening I am removing him from your care."

"We are at the poolside in the complex it's Guy's birthday. We are having a surprise birthday party, which will begin in half an hour."

"I will be over there by then. Please tell your security to let me in," Jaylee said before he could protest. "I will speak to Pete to find out what transpired over the last couple of days."

Preston hung up the phone. He felt like throwing it across the brightly lit pool deck, but he didn't. He needed the phone. It was Jaylee that he didn't need in his life.

Things would be much simpler if he had told Miss Pam that he had sex with Sheryl. At least he could have kept his baby, even if he couldn't have kept Sheryl and now he wouldn't have to be trying to adopt his son.

"There is Aunty Sheryl," Pete said eagerly.

"Aunty Sheryl?" Preston turned to the entrance of the pool area to see her. She was in a bright dress with swirls of orange and blues. Her hair was out. She looked like a young Diana Ross.

He wondered which one of his brothers invited her. Then he saw Walter go up to her and then he smiled to himself.

Walter was playing matchmaker. He had been disappointed that Sheryl had not shown up at his potluck and he was making up for it.

Preston had told him that Sheryl had looked uncomfortable around Pete and Walter was determined to fix that. Preston did not deny that it was a good strategy; she needed gradual exposure to Pete.

His five-day business trip had not helped in his strategy. He wondered if she had missed him or even noticed that he was not around. He was deliberate in not calling her after the introductions at church. He wanted her to call him.

She finished talking to Walter and was looking around the pool area. There were about thirty persons milling around. Most of them were church friends or Walter's friends. Guy had few friends; he was an introvert who did not mind spending time by himself. He was not going to like this surprise.

Preston had warned Walter, but as usual Walter, the extrovert had no problems with a party. He would have one every day if he could.

Preston turned to Pete. "You want to go and say hi to Aunty Sheryl?"

"Yes." Pete got up.

Another extrovert in the making. Preston thought as his son sauntered from the table and toward Sheryl.

He had the sneaky suspicion that Pete was the best of all of them. He was brave and bold and unafraid of most things. It had taken guts to hike from one end of Jamaica to the other to find his real family.

His son had gumption. He admired his lithe figure as he approached Sheryl and started talking to her.

He figured he should go over and join the conversation when he saw Jaylee enter the venue.

She was in a sparkly red dress and very high heels that she had difficulty walking in. Preston groaned and then got up. He didn't want Jaylee and Sheryl to meet. He didn't want Jaylee's brand of vitriol to spill over on an unsuspecting Sheryl.

Case beat him to Jaylee's side. She was now sufficiently distracted.

He passed by Sheryl and Pete.

"Hi Sheryl." he smiled at her. She was looking a lot more relaxed with Pete than at their first introduction. He was relieved to see that.

"Hello, Preston." Sheryl looked between him and Pete. "Pete was telling me about his time spent with Guy on his farm."

"He will chew your ears off about it," Preston said.

"He makes it sound so fascinating though," Sheryl said a hint of wistfulness in her voice. "A strawberry farm sounds perfect."

"We can go next week Sunday," Preston said casually, "Want to come?"

"Sure." Sheryl smiled at him. "Of course."

"Well then, it's a date."

"A date?" He heard Jaylee's acid tone behind him. "First you go away and leave Pete for five days, and now you are making dates in front of him."

"Who are you?" Jaylee demanded, she stepped around Preston and skewered Sheryl with her gaze.

"I uh," Sheryl looked between him and Jaylee, a confused look on her face, "my name is Sheryl."

"Sheryl, well excuse me," Jaylee growled. "I need to have a family meeting with Preston and Pete if that is okay with you."

Sheryl nodded. "Of course er..."

"Jaylee Bryan." Jaylee turned to Preston. "Now if you don't mind. I have a party to attend after this."

"Sure." Preston inclined his head, "will the house be all right?"

"Yes." Jaylee nodded. She tottered away heading for his house.

"Pete let her in," Preston said handing him the key.

"Okay," Pete said reluctantly. "Can I come back and chat with Aunty Sheryl some more?"

"Sure." Preston nodded.

Preston then looked at Sheryl apologetically. "Sorry about this, I will be back in a bit."

Sheryl nodded. "It's okay. I understand you have to meet with your family."

****

Sheryl craned her neck every couple of minutes to see if Preston and Pete were coming back from their family meeting.

Guy had shown up more than twenty minutes before and had looked genuinely surprised to see the gathering.

Walter had introduced them, and they had been sitting down at a corner table chit-chatting ever since. She didn't know anybody at the party and Guy was just not in the party mood. He had confessed as much to her earlier.

"I am going to punish Walter for this," he muttered. "He knows I hate parties."

"He seems like he is having fun." Sheryl chuckled at Guy's disgruntled expression.

Walter was in the limelight. His hand was thrown across an older lady's neck. He had a drink in his other hand, and he was surrounded by a few persons who seemed captivated by his presence.

Guy nodded. "He would enjoy it. He is a social butterfly, me not so much. I hate crowds. Where are Preston and Pete?"

"They are having a family meeting with Jaylee." Sheryl was happy to impart the information because she wanted to learn more about Jaylee. She assumed she was Pete's mother and Preston's ex. Obviously, she was still possessive of her family. Jaylee had emphasized the word family in letting Sheryl know that she was an outsider.

"Jaylee." Guy took a sip of his drink and then shook his head. "She is something else."

"Why did you say that?" Sheryl felt like shaking the information out of Guy. He was not very chatty. She was trying to mine information out of the wrong brother.

None of the brothers would be right for the questioning she had in mind. She realized this after Guy relaxed in his chair and started sipping his drink. They would all tell her that she should ask Preston about Jaylee.

And she would.

She especially wanted to know what Pete's relationship with his mom was. He hadn't looked particularly happy to see her. Nor had Preston for that matter. Before she herded them into the house, she had thought that they had looked a little resigned. Preston had looked annoyed.

They were obviously not on good terms, and she felt very bad about liking that. She coveted Jaylee's son. It was weird how attached she felt to Pete. Tonight he had come over and talked to her, and she had been unaccountably pleased. Almost as pleased as she was to see Preston's cleanly shaven familiar face.

She wanted Jaylee's family, and she wished that she was the one who had the authority to call a family meeting.

The last thought caught her by surprise, and she stared down at her drinks almost frightened by the thought.

"I know what you are thinking." Guy broke into her thoughts. "And you are right."

"Huh?" Sheryl looked up at him and blinked.

"I said I know what you are thinking." Guy twirled his empty cup on the table.

"I was thinking I know who is your least favorite brother of the five." Sheryl raised an eyebrow.

"Ha," Guy grinned, his whole face lit up when he laughed, "that's a nice deflection from talking about the obvious. I will play along though; I don't have a least favorite brother. I love them all. They each have some personality trait I like and some things that I don't like much, but by and large, I love them all."

"Good answer." Sheryl smiled. "But I think you have a teensy weensy bit extra for one of them."

"You got me." Guy chuckled. "I have a teensy weensy bit extra for Walter. Some years it varies, this year it's Walter."

"Walter?" Sheryl widened her eyes. "Walter who just threw you a surprise party? But you hate surprise parties."

"Yeah," Guy grinned, "this wasn't always the case mind you. But when Walter hit his twenties, he became a different person. Not that he wasn't good before. Now he is more… I don't know… deeper. And then maybe it's an age thing; we are almost the same age, so we have that in common.

"Then again it could be an opposites thing. When he is around, I don't have to work a room so hard, or maybe it's the fact that he can be a very good sounding board and I can call him up at midnight to vent. He gives good advice."

"Ah," Sheryl nodded, "I get you. Like how Preston and

Jordan were pretty tight..."

"They still are." Guy grinned. "Jordan is Preston's flamboyant twin."

"Interesting," Sheryl nodded, "very interesting. As an only child, I envy you guys. I struggled to make friends after my illness, and here you are with five ready made ones."

Guy nodded. "It almost didn't happen this way. Imagine, if Jennifer Wiley hadn't done what she did, we wouldn't be together. Probably, we would have been estranged. Who knows? I am very happy we are friends as well as brothers. Some things happen in life that immediately appear as a tragedy, but there are desirable results that can happen after it."

He cleared his throat. "Earlier when I said that I know what you are thinking, I actually do. You keep looking in the direction of the townhouse waiting for Preston to emerge. You are probably even jealous of Jaylee. You don't have to be, you know. They are over. Completely over."

Sheryl swallowed. "Really?"

"There is no hope of reconciliation there." Guy shook his head. "I'll tell you a secret, Preston has been subconsciously searching for you for the past couple of years, the Sheryl he had such a crush on when he was twelve. He probably didn't even realize it. God had set the stage for the reunion. All you have to do is be yourself. Be his friend and you'll be fine."

Guy got up. "Here he comes now."

Sheryl looked toward the townhouse. Preston was heading toward them with Pete in tow.

"I am going to go mingle," Guy said picking up his cup. "I'll probably tag along with Walter and smile and nod. People think I am wise when I do that."

Sheryl laughed. "You are wise, Guy Wiley."

****

Guy's birthday party turned out to be a good one. Sheryl thought Walter drew out party games out of his hat like a magician. He had even gotten Guy involved. Looking at him participate you couldn't tell that he had protested against the party.

She had found herself more than once cracking up as the Wiley brothers including Preston was forced to do some ridiculous things in the name of entertainment. Saint who had come late was forced to do stand up comedy. Preston, Walter, and Case did a skit about Guy's first day of high school. Even Pete was asked to sing karaoke: Forever Young, Rod Stewart. He belted out, *May the good Lord be with you down every road you roam. And may sunshine and happiness surround you when you're far from home.*

He dazzled the gathering and had them singing along to the song. She found herself acting pretty lighthearted more than her recent memories could conjure.

She was sad to see it end.

Preston walked her to her car. "And that my lady was a Walter Wiley party."

Sheryl chuckled. "I loved it."

"I am sure if you hang around us he will throw a party for you as well." Preston pushed his hand into his pocket. "So how are those dreams coming on?"

"Which dreams?" Sheryl avoided his eyes.

"The erotic ones staring the two of us?" Preston shrugged. "I am merely asking from a scientific perspective. I was away for five days. Did my absence make them go away?"

"No," Sheryl muttered. "The good news is I am sleeping through the night."

"Good." Preston looked at her meaningfully. "So that means you will be able to tackle Widcombe Heights?"

"I guess." Sheryl laughed. "I am up for it."

"Well, then tomorrow morning?" Preston asked. "I missed the exercise and the company."

"I missed you too." Sheryl found herself admitting.

"Now, that is what I want to hear." Preston grinned. "I will sleep with a smile on my face tonight."

"Night Preston," Sheryl said. "See you tomorrow."

"Night Sheryl. Sweet dreams."

Chapter Fifteen

Six weeks. Sheryl marked it on her calendar. She was in Jamaica for six weeks. She couldn't believe that she had protested coming. So far it had not been that bad. She had worked out a routine, and most of it centered on Preston and Pete. She spent her mornings with Preston; they had lunch together most days at Yum Yum. She was even settling in at church. She had been introduced to a few church members at Guy's party, and she had been to a few of Walter's potlucks.

The Wiley brothers wholeheartedly accepted her without a problem. She had even been to movie night at Case's house. Saint had introduced her to his fiancée Sandrene.

Guy had cooked for them after they visited his farm. It was an elaborate meal that she was still not convinced that he did by himself. The only fly in her ointment, her only issue with her renewed relationships so far was the fact that she had never been inside Preston's house.

She had visited most of the other brothers in their homes

but not Preston's.

It had been bugging her lately. She went to his townhouse complex to park her car every day before going on their morning walk. They had eventually made it to the top of Widcombe Heights and seen the sunrise.

She had good banter with him every morning. They spoke about nearly everything, bar the two topics that were on her no-talk list: the son that she gave up for adoption and the dream she had of her and Preston.

And the one topic that was on his list: Jaylee.

He had told her that when she was ready to talk about her son, he would talk about Jaylee. She was fine with that.

She felt as if they were in a good place, so she did not want to get into that conversation, not right now. She didn't want to feel depressed; some conversations would be guaranteed triggers. Her depressive episodes took a while to be resolved. They didn't dissipate as easily as the average person's depression, they stuck to her like glue.

She had even confessed to him, just this morning that she felt as if she had an affinity to Pete. He was just so easy to love.

Preston had gone silent on her for nearly half of the walk. Maybe she shouldn't have said that, but it was true. She loved the boy—insta love with Jaylee and Preston's son.

She should probably find her own child and see if she could make a connection with him instead of getting so attached to Pete, but the thought of searching for the child she gave away seemed like a daunting task.

First of all, she didn't know where to start looking. Her mother had been vague on that front, finally suggesting that she call the adoption board. She did. They had asked her questions like what was the child's birthday.

"January second, a day after new years day."

"Which year was he born?"

"Two thousand and one."

"Which hospital?"

"The Ford Mental Facility."

And then silence.

There was such a stigma attached to mental health that she was wondering if the person had hung up on her.

But then the lady had taken her details and said they would get back to her.

She was holding out no hopes for that.

She hit the pen on her desk rhythmically. Her mind was back on Pete again. Jaylee had no idea how blessed she was to have him as her son.

And then she frowned; there was something very odd about Jaylee and Pete's relationship. Pete didn't spend weekends with her, and on the weekdays he stayed with Preston.

She had asked Pete once how often he saw Jaylee and he had said every two weeks. Their arrangement was odd. Why would a mother voluntarily give up her son to be raised by his father and only have contact with him so infrequently? Not that she was judging, it was none of her business. Obviously, Preston and Jaylee were young when they had him.

Maybe Jaylee wanted her freedom, and Preston was better financially able to take care of Pete.

Sheryl looked at her computer where she had brought up a list of potential customers and then scrolled through slowly. For some of them, all she needed to do, was expand their distribution list. Carragon had many more products than Greenwood had offered previously.

"Hey," Noel, stuck his head around her door, "what's going on?"

"Nothing." Sheryl's tone was crisp and abrupt. She dared not soften her stance. He just needed an excuse to say something inappropriate to her.

Noel came into the room more fully. "We need to make some additions to that sales manual that head office sent down. When is a good time to run it over with me?"

"Now," Sheryl said. "I am free for a couple of hours. I have a lunch meeting."

"Client?" Noel asked, "or personal?"

Sheryl bit her lip before responding. "Both."

"I see." Noel frowned. "Is it Preston Wiley? You've been seeing a lot of him lately."

"And how would you know that?" Sheryl asked. "Are you spying on me?"

"Not actively," Noel said. "I was at Yum Yum a couple of times and saw you there with him."

"He's a friend," Sheryl said. "I like spending time with him."

"Yes, well," Noel narrowed his eyes, "it's none of my business."

"Good for you," Sheryl murmured. "It seems as if we can work together amicably after all. Shall we go into the conference room?"

Noel nodded, but she missed the look of raw jealousy that was blazing from his eyes or the tightening of his lips.

Noel was completely taken up with it. It was like a live thing. He knew he had a dog in the manger attitude. He didn't want Sheryl for himself, at least not to have a relationship though he wouldn't turn down having an affair with her. He was extremely attracted to her even though he was disgusted by her past and it bothered him that he liked her so much.

It was the highest irony that he was her boss, but that did not change the fact that he couldn't handle her past, he had tried but he couldn't. He wasn't one of those persons who could shrug away mental illness, promiscuity plus a child that she gave away for adoption.

She shouldn't have told him. He had been blissfully in love. If she didn't have so much baggage, she would have been perfect for him.

It stuck in his craw that she was finding happiness with someone else though. This poorly concealed attempt at pretending that she was just friends with this guy was bugging him. Just like it bugged him that Sheryl had not been devastated after their break up a year ago.

He wished that she had begged him to take her back, but she didn't.

It all didn't sit well with him. His ego had taken a beating, and he couldn't let it go. Sheryl should be walking around in sackcloth and ashes trying to convince him that she had changed and she was no longer the person she had been. Instead, she had moved on.

Noel could bet that she wouldn't be as confident if Preston Wiley knew her past. He didn't know much about Preston Wiley beyond what he had read in the Caribbean Financial article, but he was almost sure rich self-made good-looking men would not be interested in a woman with mental illness and promiscuity in her past.

He knew that Preston and Sheryl knew each other when they were younger, but Sheryl had probably not filled in the blanks for him.

He smiled wickedly; maybe he would and shatter Preston Wiley's illusions about her. Sheryl should be as miserable as he was. Perhaps they could comfort each other then.

"What are you smiling about?" Sheryl asked him when they reached the conference room door.

"I am just happy," Noel said. "I am contemplating something fascinating."

Sheryl turned her exotic brown eyes on him suspiciously

but didn't say a thing.

****

Preston sat down to his regular lunch at Yum Yum. He had several things to do today, but he was hoping that Sheryl would show up and they could have their regular lunchtime conversation.

He was becoming dependent on them, which was ironic because he saw her in the mornings, but that was six long hours ago.

He was very close to telling her about Pete and begging her to be a permanent fixture in their lives. He was tired of waiting for her to talk about the adoption. She already loved Pete; she said as much and Pete had taken to her like a duck to water. He was always asking about Aunt Sheryl.

He was going to give them one more month together. He even had a plan to throw them together as much as he could. Pete was not progressing as well as he should with his reading. He was going to ask Sheryl to help out.

He'd give them one month.

And then all bets were off. He was getting tired of being friends; he wanted to be more, much more.

"There you are." Jaylee came into his line of vision. And sat down across from him. She had a serious expression.

"I want you to know that I have had a change of heart."

Preston focused on her. "You have?"

Jaylee nodded. "Yes. I must confess that I have been thwarting the adoption process."

"That's a surprise," Preston murmured sarcastically, "and a real shocker."

"I know key people in the adoption process, and I have said things to stall the process." Jaylee sighed. "I made things right today. I am not comfortable playing bitch or liar or being mean. I do have a conscience, and I do pray and meditate. This whole thing is hampering my spiritual life."

"Thank God for that." Preston smiled. "I am happy that you've had a change of heart."

"I just want to know one thing." Jaylee leaned toward him conspiratorially. "Who is Pete's biological mother?"

Preston narrowed his gaze at her. "Why is that information important?"

"I was thinking about it," Jaylee said. "I couldn't believe I never thought to ask. Was she somebody you loved?"

"Yes," Preston said abruptly.

"What was her secret?" Jaylee frowned at him, "and why did she give away her child?"

"There was no secret," Preston said cryptically. "I just loved her."

"But why?" Jaylee asked plaintively, "was the sex that good?"

"I loved her since I was twelve," Preston said, "I wasn't even thinking about sex. I can't explain the mechanics of attraction or why a person would be attracted to someone above another."

Jaylee looked miffed. "Does your new girlfriend know that you still have feelings for Pete's mother?"

"I haven't told her anything." Preston raised an eyebrow. "Why all these questions?"

"Because I was just looking for closure from our relationship." Jaylee sighed. "I want to walk away from us with the assurance that there is nothing wrong with me."

"Why would you think that something was wrong with you?" Preston asked puzzled.

"You do not see this from my point of view." Jaylee shrugged. "I thought we were doing well together and then you broke up with me. It hurts but I hid my feelings. I grinned and nodded like an idiot.

"I thought something was wrong with me, but it's not. I am a desirable woman. I have a lot to offer some other unattached male, and I have no reason to keep sabotaging your adoption process. I am above that sort of petty madness."

Preston smiled. "You are a desirable woman Jaylee, and you deserve someone to love you wholeheartedly."

"Oh, I know," Jaylee smirked. "You know, you should carry around a sign saying handsome, single but unavailable emotionally. It would save another unsuspecting woman from getting hurt."

"Jaylee, come on," Preston sighed, "I was not that bad."

"You are right." Jaylee shook her head. "You were Mister Perfect until...nothing. Bam, suddenly I wasn't good enough."

"Wasn't it better to let you know before we got even deeper," Preston asked, "or would you have preferred if I strung you along?"

"I guess you have a point." Jaylee got up. "Anyway, I am going on vacation for four weeks. I do not need to check up on you so often. I was still hankering for a place in your life, but I'm cured. You are a good father to the kid. You have the means to provide for him, and you love him. I will probably call every month until the adoption is finalized."

Preston nodded. "Thank you, Jaylee. All the best."

"All the best to you as well." Jaylee picked up her bag and walked out of Yum Yum. She almost collided with Sheryl at the door.

"Oh hey, it's you." Jaylee looked at Sheryl. "I have given up on Preston. He is all yours. Hopefully, when I go on vacation to Canada, I will find someone. Be warned about Preston. He is emotionally unavailable. He will drop you like used garbage if you don't meet up to the ideal in his head."

Sheryl opened her mouth. "It's Jaylee isn't it?"

"Yes, me in the flesh." Jaylee smiled. "Good luck, you'll need it with that man."

Sheryl watched as Jaylee strode through the restaurant and out the doors. She spun around and looked at Preston who was sitting at his usual table. He was staring into space blankly.

She walked over to him and sat down.

His face lit up. "Hey, you."

"Hey." Sheryl smiled, but it didn't quite reach her eyes. *Would he drop her like garbage soon?* He was very cautious with her. He hasn't even invited her into his house. *Was Jaylee right? Am I wasting my time with Preston?*

"What's wrong?" Preston picked up on her mood almost instantly.

"Nothing," Sheryl muttered. "I just...never mind."

"You sure?" Preston asked. "Because you don't look all right."

"I am cool." Sheryl nodded. "I should go and order lunch."

"Yep." Preston nodded. "They have your favorite, fried chicken, and mashed potatoes."

Sheryl smiled. "My goodness. I love when they do that."

She got up swiftly and then went to order. While she was in the line, she wondered how she would bring up the fact that she wanted to be invited to Preston's place. Would he think that she was pushy? Maybe he still had reservations about her being around his son. He was a single dad. He couldn't be too cautious. Maybe she was overreacting.

When she got back to the table with her food Preston grinned at her. "You were always a sucker for that meal."

"You remembered?" Sheryl inhaled the aroma from her food dramatically and then grinned before digging in.

"I was wondering," Preston said slowly, "would you like to help Pete with his reading if it is not too much of an imposition? I could, but some evenings I reach home too late to be consistent..."

Sheryl started nodding before he could continue. "Yes, I could. At your house?"

"Yes," Preston nodded, "if it won't be a problem."

"It won't." Sheryl couldn't stop the grin that spread across her face. "Any book in particular that you want me to use?"

"Guy bought him a bunch of books." Preston looked at her gratefully, "You can use anyone you feel like using."

"I should give you this." He pushed a bunch of keys and a gate opener toward her. "Those are your keys to my place. "

"Your place?" Sheryl whispered scooping them up.

"Yes." Preston gave her a mock glare. "Don't lose them."

Sheryl curled her hands around them. "This is unexpected. The doors to your inner sanctum. I don't know what to say."

"When you come by tomorrow morning I will give you a tour," Preston said somberly.

Chapter Sixteen

Sheryl drove to Preston's townhouse half convinced that their lunch yesterday was part of a prank, and a set up for today, April fool's day.

She feared that she would reach the complex, press the gate opener and a little flag would appear at the top with a grinning head.

She tentatively touched the little black gadget and was surprised when the black gate slid back into the wall.

She drove through and parked in front of Preston's house. She got out and stretched. It was still early. Usually, Preston would be waiting for her outside. This time she let herself through his front door.

"Anybody home?" She whispered as she pushed the door opened.

"Just us." Preston appeared in the kitchen doorway. He was already in his jogging outfit. He looked like a model from one of those fitness magazines especially when he gave her that slow once over smile.

"Pete said he wants to come walking with us, so I am waiting for him to put on his sneakers. Want me to give you a tour in the meantime?"

"Er...yes." Sheryl was almost sure that this was an extended dream. She had dreamt about this last night. Maybe she wasn't really here, and it was an extended version of it.

"Come on in," he said casually as if this was not a momentous occasion. He had given her keys to his house. He had given her his gate opener. Did he realize that this was a huge deal? Or maybe she was overreacting, and he did this all the time?

"You are the first female to get the house tour apart from Shawn that is," Preston said as if he were reading her mind. "She designed the place, so she gave me the tour and told me how to furnish the place, of course."

Sheryl smiled. "I can imagine her doing that. It would be nice to see Shawn all grown up."

"She'll be here for Saint's rehearsal dinner and then the wedding," Preston murmured, "It is in early May."

"I haven't forgotten that this is your birth month." Sheryl smiled. "I remember you hating your birthdays. How has it been for you these past couple of years?"

"I try to do good stuff on the day." Preston looked at her solemnly. "Do you remember twelve years ago, on my birthday when your mother dragged you into the living room and declared that you were pregnant and one of us had better marry you?"

"It's too early to talk about that." Sheryl frowned, "and yes I can vaguely remember that event."

Preston stood in front of her. "When are you going to want to talk about this?"

"I don't know." Sheryl swallowed. "Someday. I feel

pretty guilty and ashamed of it, you know. It's the kind of conversation that I want to avoid."

"And you don't fully trust me yet," Preston said bending his head and kissing her briefly on the lips.

Sheryl gasped. Her lips had instantly started getting tingly.

"It's not that I don't trust you," Sheryl whispered. "It's just that I don't want to talk about it."

"Okay," Preston said stepping back. "Let's get on with the tour."

They walked through the tastefully decorated place slowly; they even looked into Pete's room. He was putting on his sneakers.

"Aunty Sheryl!" His face lit up when he saw her. "Did Dad tell you I am coming with you this morning?

"Yes," Sheryl smiled, "I am looking forward to seeing if you can make it up that hill easily." "Of course." Pete stood up hurriedly. "I have walked up steeper hills."

"Oh really?" Sheryl asked.

"I did it while hungry too," Pete said grinning. "This will be a piece of cake."

Sheryl assumed that he was talking about a Blue Mountain trek or something.

Preston showed her the rest of upstairs. She paused in his room. Surprisingly, it was not as masculine as she thought it would be. It was painted in white with a turquoise accent wall, a large painting of the Blue Lagoon in Portland hung over his bed. It complimented the room's decor. She glanced at him quickly. That had been her favorite color for years. *Did he realize that?*

She leaned on the doorjamb. "Your room is girly."

"Dark turquoise is not girly." Preston leaned on the opposite jamb from her. "I thought you would like it."

"I do," Sheryl murmured, "but I am confused."

"No need to be," Preston looked at her naked pink lips longingly. "You know that song is true? The first cut is the deepest."

"What does that mean?" Sheryl frowned.

"I never recovered from my first cut. You work it out." Preston grinned. "Your assignment, Miss Stone."

Sheryl stared at him as Pete joined him and they headed down the stairs.

"You coming?" Preston laughed at her slack-jawed expression.

"Er...yes," Sheryl muttered.

****

Two weeks later, Sheryl was sitting and listening to Pete read the book Escape To Last Man Peak by Jean D'costa. This was their third book on her top three list. She had chosen the books the moment she had seen it in Guy's box of interesting books.

So many of them brought back memories of her childhood, Escape to Last Man Peak in particular. She had loved it as a girl. She remembered reading it when she had lived with her mother in Portland before her life had taken a turn for the worse.

She wanted Pete to read it to her again and to love the whole reading process. So far he was doing more than great. He was reading even without her. Sometimes he flew ahead with the story preferring to tell her about where he had left off the next day. He was going to be just fine. To be honest, he didn't need her anymore.

She was staring at him as he looked down in the book and she had the weirdest sensation that she was looking at Preston as a boy. He was so achingly familiar. Was that the reason she felt so maternal towards him?

But that was rubbish; she didn't feel maternal towards Preston. Not in the least. Her hormones were back in overdrive. Preston just had to look at her, and she was in a very uncomfortable state of arousal.

Her nightly dreams had taken on even more of an erotica quality, and she saw details and felt sensations she was sure was just a result of her overactive imagination. She had not had sex in twelve years her sexuality was just waking up again, and it was because of Preston.

She was at their house more than she was at her apartment. She was viewing it as her personal domain, and Preston let her. He encouraged it.

She had taken over fixing supper for her and Pete until Preston got home around seven or so, then he would join them. After Pete went to bed, they would sit and talk and share about their day. But then she would have to go home. She was beginning to hate that.

She was getting too attached.

She had all but forgotten about Jaylee's warning.

Jaylee who was gone on vacation she had taken over the woman's family.

What if Preston dropped her like a hot potato?

She had listened to the song, the first cut is the deepest over and over, and she was a bit disquieted. Was Jaylee Preston's first? Had she gotten the best of him and he was trying to tell her that he would try to love again?

The thought had her biting her lip. She hadn't even realized that Pete had stopped reading and was staring at her.

"I wish you were my mom." His voice intruded on her thoughts like a slam.

She focused on him. "Say that again?"

"I just wish you were my mom," Pete repeated shyly. "I

like having you around. My dad loves having you around. I wish you lived with us."

"I...er..." Sheryl swallowed, "I love being with you too Pete."

Pete nodded and then looked down at his book. "These children in Escape To Last Man Peak were orphans. I know what that feels like."

"Pete," Sheryl looked at him and frowned, "you have Preston and Jaylee."

Pete nodded. "I know, I love my dad. I just miss having a mom."

Uh oh, Jaylee's absence was making the boy unhappy. Sheryl didn't know if she should be grateful to the woman for leaving her family for her to get a foothold or ask Preston to talk to her to spend more time with her own child.

She got up and kissed Pete on his forehead. "I tell you what, I can be your friend whatever happens between me and your father. Anytime you want me; I'll come running. I'll do anything for you."

"Thank you, Aunty Sheryl," Pete beamed at her. "I think I love you."

"I know I love you," Sheryl said with a certainty that was both puzzling and scary at the same time. She had never been surer. There was a special place in her heart for him, and it was growing bigger and bigger the more exposed she was to him.

****

Sheryl called Preston two days later to cancel her regular lunchtime with him. She had a meeting with Noel and a prominent distributor.

Preston usually expected her to show up. If she didn't, he would have a little panic attack. Sheryl smiled to herself as she dialed his number. She couldn't get him on his cell phone. She called his office instead.

Helena came on the phone. She was used to Helena by now. They even had little chats before she put her through to Preston. The last conversation was about what present to get Preston for his birthday.

"Give to his favorite charity, the boys home," Helena had said, in his name. "That is the only present that makes him happy."

Helena sounded glum today though. "You just missed him, Sheryl," she said when she recognized Sheryl's voice. "He had to rush home, Pete is ill."

"Ill?" Sheryl squeaked. Her heart started a panicked erratic beat, "What's wrong with him?"

"I don't know, he had a fever and is feeling low."

"But I saw him when we went walking this morning, and he was fine. Well a little sluggish," Sheryl amended. "We were teasing him that he could barely make it up the hill."

Sheryl got up from her desk, "I am going over there."

"I didn't expect anything less," Helena murmured, a smile in her voice. "Tell the boss I have everything under control here. I canceled all his meeting today. You two concentrate on your...I mean Pete's health."

Sheryl hung up. Worry was creasing her face. She was panicking for no reason. Pete probably had a mild childhood sickness.

She headed to Noel's office and knocked briefly on the door. "I have an emergency I can't be at the meeting."

"What type of emergency?" Noel asked. He was on his computer a look of intense concentration on his face. "Jamal Linton is almost as important as the Wiley account."

"I know, and I am sorry, but there is a sick little boy that needs me right now," Sheryl said before she could stop herself. "I am out. Make my apologies."

She stepped away from the door before she could hear what Noel said.

Traffic had never been as annoying to her as it was today. It seemed as if every red light caught her. She finally reached The Wiley's an hour later, and she could hardly wait to jam the car into park before she was out of it and letting herself into Preston's house.

Preston was talking to a man in the kitchen area.

"Sheryl, is everything all right?" he looked at her concerned.

"No!" Sheryl said breathlessly. "I just heard that Pete was ill. Where is he? How bad is it?"

"Not bad." The man beside Preston said. "I am Trey King, Preston's friend, and doctor and you are?"

"Sheryl." Sheryl shook his proffered hand.

The doctor glanced at Preston and then turned to her, "Sheryl? The Sheryl? Well, it's nice to meet you."

Sheryl nodded impatiently. "About Pete, what's wrong?"

Trey grinned before he responded. "Don't worry, Pete has gastroenteritis a very mild manifestation of it. You need to replenish the liquids he is losing and monitor him closely. I won't recommend any medications at this time but if it gets worse in the next three days, give me a call."

Preston saw Dr. King to the door, and Sheryl went to check up on Pete.

He was lying in a fetal-like position. His little face looked woebegone. Her heart melted. Pete looked up at her with sick glazed eyes.

"Aunty Sheryl?"

"I am here baby," Sheryl said. She didn't care that she was overreacting she kicked off her shoes and curled up beside him, hugging him close.

Chapter Seventeen

"**S**he spent all night with him," Preston whispered to Saint, Walter, Case, and Guy who had gathered downstairs with concern stamped on their faces.

"She is like a single-minded mother hen who is taking care of her chick. She hardly slept, and she is not eating. I am heading to her apartment to get her a change of clothes. She won't leave him. She said she promised him to stay."

"Goodness," Walter whispered, "she is acting like his mother."

"She is his mother." Guy chuckled, "and she doesn't even know."

"She knows subconsciously," Walter added, she is working off instincts right now. "Her child is hurting, and she will not rest until he is better."

"You should tell her," Saint said, "but not now. Wait until he gets better. If she finds out she is his mother now, she will be an emotional mess."

"Right." Preston nodded. "Thank you all for your advice. I have to go."

"We'll be here when you get back," Walter muttered. "I hope Sheryl will let us see Pete."

"Before you go, can we decide who is picking up Jordan from the airport this evening?" Case said. "I have a cooperate event tonight, so I might not be able to go."

"I'll do it, Guy said, I am free tonight."

"Okay." Preston looked at his brothers. "I'll be back soon."

He got in the car and sat in there for a full minute. He had never been able to handle sick children very well. He outwardly seemed calm, but inside he was an emotional mess. He had gone through it with Case and to a lesser extent with Saint especially because they were the youngest.

When Case was eleven, he had gotten bronchial pneumonia. Preston still remembered the terror he had felt when he had thought that his baby brother, who was under his care, was going to die.

He had been so panic-stricken at the time that he had been almost comatose with it. And now, there was Pete, not just a brother, but his own son.

His and Sheryl's.

Sheryl had effortlessly stepped into her role as mother as if she was born for it. Sheryl who was calm and caring and held his panic at bay.

He heaved a sigh. They made a good team. These past couple of weeks he had assessed her. He had been working on a way to tell her that he could not see himself living without her. And he would tell her shortly. His birthday was in a week, he would propose then.

It was on his birthday twelve years ago that Miss Pam had announced to them that Sheryl was pregnant, it would be only fitting that he made things right on his birthday this year. God knew that many unhappy things happen on his birthday. He would make sure that an outstandingly good thing happened this year.

Maybe this was the year to finally meet his birthday with anticipation.

He started the car and headed through the gates, a smile on his face.

****

Sheryl didn't know what time it was when she finally fell into an uncomfortable sleep in Preston's guest room.

She had sleepily chatted to Preston's brothers after they checked on Pete and then had called in at the office and told them she wasn't coming in. She was almost sure she would get the lambasting of her life from Noel, but she didn't care now. Pete was on the mend.

At least that was what she had gathered from his peaceful expression when she had woken up at one o'clock to check on Pete. Preston had forced her to eat some soup, and they had a conversation, which she could barely remember. He said something about her getting her rest and not running herself ragged.

And then she had gone to sleep herself.

It was night now. She woke up groggily and saw a travel bag that looked like hers at the end of the bed. Preston had said something about collecting her stuff too and that he would cook them dinner if she was up.

She yawned and padded into the en-suite bathroom. The clock on the wall said eight o'clock.

She felt stiff and achy as if she needed to exercise to work out some of the kinks. She had spent most of the night curled up to Pete. That had been the only thing that seemed to keep him calm.

She turned on the shower, stepped under the spray and closed her eyes. She didn't need a therapist to tell her that she was transferring all her pent up motherly instincts onto Pete.

Maybe it was unhealthy, but it didn't feel that way to her. She knew for certain right now that she loved that boy and she would do anything to see him get better soon.

And she didn't want to think about not being in his life or Preston's for that matter.

She padded back into the room pulled on one of the casual dresses that Preston had packed for her. She looked at her pile of underwear in her bag. She could imagine him hovering over them and then just choosing a handful.

She chuckled to herself.

Pete was up when she went to his room. Preston was feeding him soup.

"Hey, you two." She stood at the doorjamb and watched them.

Preston looked handsome, delicious enough to eat. He was clean-shaven; he had rolled up his dress shirt to his elbow and was in a pair of very faded blue jeans that fit him perfectly.

"Hey." He turned to her and smiled.

Pete looked brighter when he turned to her. "Aunty Sheryl, Daddy said I couldn't have ice cream."

"Daddy is right." Sheryl smiled. "You'll have to wait a couple of days to put dairy in your tummy."

"He is on the mend," Preston said, "whatever it was that caused him to react like that is now out of his system, I presume so or else he wouldn't be asking for ice cream."

"I feel so tired," Pete said half closing his eyes.

"That's because you need to rest. So that your body can do its healing thing." Preston said softly. He wiped Pete's lips. "Go to sleep."

"Will aunty Sheryl be here?" Pete whispered, his voice thread-like.

"I'll be here," Sheryl whispered. "Just ring the bell if you want something."

"Okay." Pete slid back under the covers and was out like a light.

"Now it's your time to get fed." Preston stood up. "Miss Blossom made dinner."

Sheryl nodded. "I am starving. What did she make?"

"Baked chicken and quinoa salad." Preston smiled, "and she made some mini strawberry cheesecake things that she says are the best tasting cakes you will ever eat."

"Well then, let's go eat." Sheryl headed straight for the kitchen ahead of Preston.

He had already set the table in the breakfast nook and laid out the dishes buffet style.

It smelled good, as she had anticipated.

There was music on; she hadn't noticed the speakers in the kitchen ceiling before. The music added a charming intimacy to the space.

Jefferson Starship, Miracles came on. She started humming to the song, *if only you believe in miracles so would I...*

"I believe in miracles," Preston said behind her.

Sheryl spun around and grinned. "This is my jam. How did you know?"

"I didn't." Preston shrugged. "That's Miss Blossom's CD. Let's eat; I am starving."

"And probably tired." Sheryl shared out her food, "you didn't sleep much last night did you?"

"Nope." Preston shrugged. "I couldn't."

"It's stressful seeing your child sick, huh?"

"Oh definitely." Preston looked at her contemplatively. "You have really stepped in with Pete, thank you very much.

I appreciate it."

"It's no problem." Sheryl sighed, "I didn't mind. Have you told Jaylee that he is ill?"

"No," Preston frowned, "I don't want her to come back from her vacation and accuse me of being a bad parent. She would probably want to remove Pete from my care. I don't trust her to be impartial. She says she is over us, but I am not sure I want to risk her wrath."

Sheryl nodded. "I understand."

Preston started eating. "Are you sure? Because there is something I have to tell you this past couple of weeks I have been trying to work up to telling you this and I think that now is the time for us to clear the air. I was going to wait for my birthday but..."

Sheryl leaned forward her fork stuck mid-air. "I am really not interested in you and Jaylee's relationship Preston. You said it is in the past and I believe you."

"But it's not about Jaylee," Preston sighed. "Maybe we should eat first."

"Okay," Sheryl smiled at him. "Good idea."

She began eating again, obviously uncomfortable with the topic.

"Jordan is here," Preston said changing the conversation because it was obviously needed. Sheryl got defensive whenever he brought up motherhood or Jaylee. "He came two weeks before the wedding as promised."

"He is here in Jamaica?" Sheryl widened her eyes. "How nice."

"Yep." Preston grinned. "Saint would kill him if he didn't attend. His Dubai project is finished, but he is contemplating taking on another one there."

"And you hate that, because you want him here," Sheryl said shrewdly.

"I do." Preston shrugged. "Who can blame me. I like having him around."

"So Saint is going to have five groomsmen or four?" Sheryl chuckled, "how did he choose which one of you to be his best man?"

"He didn't. His best friend, Max is going to be his best man."

"Oh, you guys have outside friends?" Sheryl widened her eyes. "How intriguing."

"We are not a closed community of brothers." Preston chuckled. "Yes, we do reach outside of the tribe and include others."

"Who would you choose for your best man?" Sheryl asked.

"Jordan," Preston said without a pause.

"I rest my case." Sheryl snickered. "Tell me about Saint's wedding."

"It will be in a restaurant courtyard. It's quite lovely. The bride's parents own the restaurant. They host weddings and other parties there quite frequently. You are invited to the wedding rehearsal, which takes place on my birthday."

"I accept." Sheryl nodded. "That would be nice. Your birthday is in two days. You excited?"

"In previous years I would say no, but I am looking forward to my birthday this year with more anticipation than dread. Mainly because you are here."

"I am happy to hear that." Sheryl touched his hand. "I remember the first year after your parent's death when Jordan brought over that letter from your father."

"Yep. I still have that letter." Preston smiled, "I haven't read it in a while, but I still have it."

"Do you still feel sad every year?" Sheryl steepled her hand under her chin. "I remember how you would get."

"No, not sad, just slightly anxious. Some years are worse

than some." Preston grimaced. "I normally wake up with a knot in my chest. One year, I forgot it was my birthday, believe it or not. I woke up the morning with a sense of impending doom but then I went to work, and somebody wished me a happy birthday. I was relieved that the feeling was normal, natural for the day."

"Do you ever think about your mom?" Sheryl asked. "I mean, she is the reason for all of this."

"I do think about her." Preston sat back in his chair with a sigh. "I miss her sometimes too. I try to remember the good times though those memories are pretty sketchy. She was a great mother when she was good."

Sheryl whistled. "And terrible when she was terrible."

"That's right." Preston frowned. "She lost her head there for a while."

"I know what that is like." Sheryl toyed with her glass. "That's the only way I console myself about the adoption. I wouldn't have been the best mother to my child in that state."

Preston nodded. "It was for the best."

Sheryl cleared her throat. "How on earth did we end up talking about this. I was talking about Saint's wedding..."

Preston opened his mouth to protest. This was precisely what he was hoping that they would talk about. Adoption and motherhood and mental problems.

"What's the name of the restaurant?" Sheryl asked before he could get a word out in protest.

"Waterfalls." Preston sighed. "I can pick you up at seven."

"I am looking forward to it." Sheryl smiled. "Tell me more about the wedding."

Preston sighed. "Okay, I'll let that slide for now, but you will have to talk about it soon."

"The wedding, Preston." Sheryl leaned forward and

grinned, "or at least Saint's in-laws. Sandrene seems nice, a bit on the quiet side."

"The in-laws?" Preston grimaced, "Sandrene has a twin sister who is a party planner. Her name is Gracie, and she is somewhat of an acquired taste. Very flashy and flamboyant, twenty pounds of fake hair, five inches of fake lashes. She has nails so long I would hate to see what's under them and she dresses suggestively to show off her surgically enhanced curves."

"Ooh," Sheryl raised an eyebrow, "you don't like her. I have never heard you describe somebody with such scathing dislike."

"I don't like her." Preston sighed. "Unfortunately, she is very close to Sandrene, and I fret that Sandrene might have inherited a little bit of Gracie's er...over the top ways. I don't want her to unleash that on my brother. "

"I met Sandrene at Guy's party." Sheryl nodded, "she seemed like a nice, normal, and likable girl."

"Which is a miracle," Preston growled. "Gracie has taken over the plans for this wedding. Inviting more people than the couple would like and adding more expensive features just for the hell of it. Even the invitations were over the top. She had jewel brooches on them."

Sheryl laughed. "You should see your face when you said jewel brooches, maybe Sandrene likes bling."

"She doesn't wear jewelry." Preston quirked his lips. "I think she would much prefer something a lot more scaled down and more relaxed."

"Her sister is probably planning with herself in mind." Sheryl bit into her succulent baked chicken. "Or maybe Sandrene is secretly a bling lover, and she is not showing it."

"Either of those scenarios could be right." Preston nodded. "Tell me what you would want for your wedding."

"Me?" Sheryl smiled. "I am partial to something on the beach, just close friends, and family. I don't have many friends and definitely none out here."

"So you would get married in Jamaica?" Preston asked watching her intently.

"Of course," Sheryl said and then caught herself. "Oh my goodness, I am not sending you any signals."

She held her head and groaned. "I am not begging to...oh lord..."

Preston watched her and then chuckled. "Would you like dessert now?"

"I can't hold my head up." Sheryl whispered, "I couldn't swallow another bite. You think I am probably hankering for you to propose to me. I kinda know that it's a stretch."

"Why would it be a stretch?" Preston touched her hand.

Sheryl looked at their hands and then sighed. "I had a mental illness. I was out of my mind for a while. That's not the kind of thing I expect you would embrace even if you like me. I mean, your family history should have you running from me. What if I morph into your mother?"

"My mother?" Preston widened his eyes. "My mother was unstable because of my father. She drove herself crazy over a situation that she had no business being involved in. And I am never going to be my father. I made up my mind a long time ago to have one relationship at a time."

"But what if you decide that you loved Jaylee?" Sheryl asked. "I mean you have a lovely son with her. You already have a family."

"Okay, we are going to talk about this," Preston growled, "once and for all. You are going to hear this whether you like it or not..."

The doorbell rang, and he got up. "Hold that thought. I have something to say about your past, and you are going to listen."

Sheryl looked up at him. "Do I have to hear this?"

"Oh yes, you do. We are long overdue for this conversation."

Chapter Eighteen

"**I** took a nap before coming over." Jordan was leaning on the doorjamb when Preston answered.

Preston grinned. "You are a sight for sore eyes, little brother."

He enveloped Jordan in a bear hug and patted him on the back. "I am happy you are home."

"Me too," Jordan said," though I am sad to hear that my nephew is not well."

"Yes," Preston stepped back, "come on in. Sheryl and I were just eating."

"I heard Sheryl was here." Jordan lowered his voice, "Guy told me that she doesn't know about Pete."

"No." Preston shook his head. "She doesn't."

"This is so interesting." Jordan chuckled, "I'll not be staying long. I'll just say hi to Sheryl, look in on my nephew and be on my way. We can catch up later."

"Sure." Preston lead the way into the kitchen. As usual, he

felt a pinprick of jealousy when Sheryl reacted to one of his brothers.

He watched as she greeted Jordan hugging him too tightly for his liking.

And then she stepped back. "My Gosh, you could be Pete's father. He looks so much like the both of you. I had forgotten how closely you and Preston resembled each other."

"Oh no, I couldn't be Pete's father." Jordan turned to Preston, "definitely not, do not let the thought even cross your mind."

"It never did." Preston chuckled as he looked at Jordan's expression of horror. "I have a DNA test which says he is 99.99% mine."

Sheryl laughed. "Sorry to insinuate that you would have a thing with Jaylee."

"Jaylee?" Jordan looked confused, and then he sorted it out in his mind. "Oh, no. I had no contact with Jaylee whatsoever."

The truth is he had never met the woman.

"So how are you, Sheryl?" Jordan looked her over. "You have turned into a beauty. Not that you weren't before. Preston used to always call you his model but adult Sheryl is a sight to see."

"Shut it," Preston said through gritted teeth.

"So you haven't told her how you used to draw pictures of her in your schoolbook and drool over them, putting a darker ring around her irises and calling them mahogany eyes."

"I forgot about this, but when Preston thought that you had died during that accident, he cried like a baby. Every night he prayed, please God bring Sheryl back to me."

"Get out." Preston said, "leave us."

Sheryl was grinning from ear to ear. "No, actually I didn't know all of this, Jordan. I wish you would stay."

"The boy was a fool for you and the man is worse." Jordan chuckled, "He didn't even know it was you in the restaurant when he initially saw you again and he spent all day obsessing over the mystery girl in the restaurant…how she made him feel again. How he wished he had gone over to her and asked for her number."

Preston groaned. "I am rethinking having you as my best friend."

"That's understandable now that Sheryl is around. I guess I can take second chair and be good with that." Jordan laughed. "That's how it should be anyway."

"Don't let him play cool with you," Jordan turned to Sheryl. "He is wired to love you. I am going to look in on Pete, and then I'll get out as the gentleman says."

He gave them a salute and then left the kitchen.

Sheryl looked at Preston with a grin. "Is any of what he just said true?"

"Yes." Preston nodded. "Very true."

Sheryl walked over to Preston until they were almost touching nose to nose.

"So you do like me," Sheryl said softly, "I was beginning to wonder."

"I've loved you since the first moment I saw you," Preston whispered. "You were eleven, you had two braids in your hair, you looked at me and I felt funny. My twelve-year-old heart had just been hit by something catastrophic, and it never healed. It only got stronger. It never died, it just went dormant."

"Even with my illness?" Sheryl whispered.

"Even then." Preston sighed. "And I think that I should tell you something about that time. I don't want you to hate me."

"I couldn't hate you." Sheryl looked at him weirdly. "What could you have done that was so bad?"

"That dream you have of us," Preston said, "It's true. It happened. I don't know what you remember because you don't want to tell me but..."

"Are you serious?" Sheryl looked at him mortified. "We had sex?"

"Yes." Preston inhaled, "you came to my room one night—stark naked. I couldn't believe it, at first I thought you weren't real but you slid under the sheets, and then you started to caress..."

"Stop." Sheryl closed her eyes. "Oh my goodness. I remember what happened vividly. I was like a wild animal. I was all over you. I was biting and licking you and..."

Preston smiled. "I have vivid dreams of it as well. It was unforgettable. All your inhibitions were down; you were like every man's dream. "

Sheryl backed away from him. "I can't listen to anymore."

"Oh come on Sheryl," Preston said frustration creeping into his voice. "We are adults we can talk about this rationally."

"My mother was right. I did sleep with anyone that could walk. Do you blame me for not wanting to revisit that time in my life?"

"How many dreams do you have of other encounters?" Preston asked.

"Just the one with you," Sheryl whispered. "I managed to block out everything else it would seem."

"Maybe because you and I count for something. It was meaningful to you on a subconscious level. I don't even know why I am justifying because what we did was not the way it should have happened but..."

"I think I am going home now." Sheryl inhaled tremulously. "I can't handle all of this right now. I would like if we never spoke about it again. I am not a prude obviously, but I just hate talking about that time. Can you see where I am coming from?"

Preston said, "Sheryl, we share a very healthy amount of guilt over that night. You may have been mentally unstable, but I wasn't. I knew what I was doing, and I...we seriously need to talk some more about this."

"I know, I do." Sheryl murmured, "but now, I have to psyche myself up to talk of the past. The last person I told couldn't handle it. He looked at me as if I were a monster and I..."

"Your former fiancé?" Preston asked. "The guy you now work for?"

"Yep." Sheryl nodded.

"But we are different." Preston ran his hand over his face, "Sheryl I am a part of that past, and if you would just let us talk about it instead of hiding in your shell, we could get past a lot of this and move on."

"Sure we'll talk," Sheryl said vaguely, avoiding eye contact with him and backing out of the room like a guilty criminal. "Er...I'll call tomorrow see how Pete is doing. I have to go."

She left before Jordan. She didn't even take her things that he had gotten from her house. She drove out of the complex like someone was pursuing her.

Preston was sitting in the living room in the semi-dark when Jordan came down and sat beside him. "Is it my fault?"

"Nope," Preston whispered, "I told her that the erotic dream she was having of us was real. She panicked."

Jordan sighed. "She is no longer mentally unstable is she?"

"No." Preston frowned. "Why do you ask?"

"Just concerned." Jordan massaged his temples. "That could be an issue, but then again who am I to judge all of us rest on a tenuous line of sanity. It doesn't take much for some of us to be pushed off the edge."

"That's a unique way to look at it," Preston murmured.

"How is Pete?"

"Fast asleep." Jordan chuckled. "He is all Wiley, that boy. Joseph Wiley lives on to another generation. I am happy Pete found you. It was the perfect coincidence."

"It was too perfect to be a coincidence. It was a miracle." Preston sighed. "That boy upstairs is a living breathing miracle. It could have gone any other way, you know. He could have chosen the wrong supermarket to take something from. They would have just called child services and got him off the street and back into the system."

"Instead he is here with you just when his biological mother is actually on the scene and you three can finally get to be a proper family."

"If only it were that easy." Preston exhaled raggedly. "If her reaction to hearing that we that we slept together was so bad, imagine how she will react when she finds out that Pete is her son."

"She'll deal with it, and you'll both live happily ever after with your carbon copy child. The end." Jordan chuckled.

Preston laughed with him. "I see you are now subscribing to fairy tales."

"Nope," Jordan murmured, "but that's how I would want it to go because I love you and I want to see you happy. And I know you love her and she for some reason has always been the one to make your little heart do somersaults."

"Just like Shawn is the one who makes yours do somersaults," Preston murmured, "You two are something else. You should just marry Shawn and get it over and done with it already. You two are not just best friends. It's obvious for even the blind to see."

"Hrmph," Jordan muttered, "I don't know. I might just renew that contract in Dubai. Shawn is threatening to stop talking to me if I do."

"Because she wants to settle down with you and you are giving her no indication that you want the same." Preston turned on the side lamp and shook his head at Jordan. "Why are you being deliberately obtuse?"

"I am not." Jordan shrugged. "I am not sure that I want to settle down as you call it. My life is fine right now. I get to do stuff, travel, have adventures. Having a wife and children is just not my thing yet."

"Jordan the adventurer," Preston muttered. "You are going to lose that girl. Marry her and have your adventure together. She is your ride-or-die, remember?"

"Before things got weird between us." Jordan groaned. "We are not the same as we used to be."

"Because you both grew up." Preston frowned. "That's simple logic."

"Nah," Jordan groaned, "you don't understand. A couple years ago...never mind. I can't go into that now but...yes, Shawn and I have issues."

"Ah." Preston nodded. "Issues."

"Are they the kind of issues that Sheryl and I had?"
Jordan sighed. "No."

"But you two are still friends," Preston said confused. "You designed this place together; you still talk every day."

"That's because we are friends and I make an effort not to forget that. Anyways, she called me when I was half asleep earlier. She is coming for the rehearsal, and she is staying at my place, and she is bringing a friend. You won't be the only one with an adventurous weekend ahead."

Chapter Nineteen

"**Y**ou know you should be taking it easy." Preston looked at Pete as he scarfed down the scrambled eggs and plantain that Jordan had made for breakfast.

Today was his birthday and the all-important rehearsal dinner.

All the Wiley brothers were out en masse in his kitchen, and they had cooked up quite a spread. More food than he was willing to eat. He was a green protein smoothie in the morning kind of guy.

According to Walter, it was a breakfast party. He had brought over muffins; one of them had a candle in the middle.

"I know you hate your birthdays, and through the years you may have had good reason, but this morning there is a lot to be thankful for," Walter said. "You are alive, Pete is almost better after a brief illness, we are all together this morning of April 26, and we are all in one piece."

"Let's take a moment to appreciate these blessings and then you can start complaining that we always try too hard for your birthday yadda yadda yadda."

Preston chuckled. "I will not complain today, and thank you all for coming over."

"We had to," Guy said. "We heard that our favorite nephew is on the mend, we had to see for ourselves."

Pete stopped eating and looked at Preston. "Daddy, why don't you like to celebrate your birthday?"

"Because your grandmother spoiled it for him," Jordan said before Preston could answer.

"My grandmother, Pamela Stone?" Pete asked curiously.

"Not that grandmother, the other one," Jordan said. "Jennifer Riddley Wiley."

"May her soul rest in pieces," Walter murmured.

"Don't say that," Guy said. "It is terrible what happened, but she was still your mom. She did something good, she had you three, and I wouldn't want to change any of you for the world."

"Besides, I don't think we should tell Pete about this particular piece of family history today. Let's have a good day and celebrate Preston's birthday and Saint's rehearsal dinner and Shawn's arrival."

"Shawn is here?" Jordan was the first to react to Guy's speech.

"Yep. She just let herself into your house with a very beefy looking fellow in tow."

"Her friend is a man?" Jordan asked heading to the kitchen window to look through to see what Guy was talking about.

"That's how she likes them." Walter chuckled. "Shawn will always be more comfortable around males than females."

Everybody chuckled, but Jordan did not find it funny. He had thought that Shawn's friend would have been female, not a guy.

"I should go over there," Jordan said.

"No need, she is coming with Mr. Beefcake behind her." Guy whistled. "He looks like he could bench-press you into tomorrow."

Preston and the others went to the window.

"He could take you, Walter." Preston chuckled.

"He's twice Walter's size," Saint grunted. "Wow, he looks like Duane the rock Johnson from his WWE days."

"Or the Scorpion King movie," Case breathed. "Look at those veins in his arms and why is he so shiny?"

"Now we know how your breakfast will get eaten." Saint chuckled.

Preston looked at Shawn whose long chunky curls were glistening in the sun. "And nobody is commenting on how good Shawn looks. What an oversight."

"That's because we know how Jordan gets if you say anything even remotely nice about Shawn." Case snorted. "I learned my lesson a long time ago. As far as I am concerned Shawn is asexual."

Preston chuckled. "I got my warning when we were fourteen. I still won't listen to him. Shawn is a gorgeous woman and should be admired."

Jordan gritted his teeth. "I wish you hadn't invited her to your wedding, Saint."

"How could I not?" Saint whispered. "Shawn is family. She is practically my sister."

Preston nodded. "That's right, and she would kill you if she wasn't invited. Let me go and get the door."

Preston opened the door before Shawn could use the buzzer and was almost pushed down by Shawn's exuberant hug. "Hey, Pressy, happy birthday."

The hug was typical Shawn.

"I knew you all would be over here because it's birthday morning." Shawn gave him a sound kiss on his cheek and then stood back. "You look fab. Where is the boy, my surprise nephew?"

"In the kitchen with the rest of the clan." Preston indicated with his head.

"Come on Carl," Shawn said to the guy behind her, "let's get you introduced to my other family. This is Preston."

"Good morning." Carl nodded to Preston who nodded back.

The guy was even more overpowering close-up.

Preston closed the door and headed for the kitchen behind Shawn and Carl.

Shawn squealed when she saw Pete. "Oh my goodness, you look like Preston as a kid. This is surreal. You didn't even get a thing for Sheryl. It's as if she didn't donate any biological material to your make up at all."

Pete looked at Shawn in surprise.

Preston groaned. "I haven't told him yet. I intended to do this privately."

"Oops." Shawn clamped her hand over her mouth. "Hi Pete, I am your aunt, Shawn. And as you can hear, I talk too much."

Shawn went over and hugged him.

"Hello, Aunty Shawn." Pete hugged her back.

"Aunt Sheryl is my mother? Pete asked looking from one uncle to the other and then back to his father. "But how?"

"The usual way, there was a stork, haven't you heard the story?"

"He is eleven." Preston groaned, "When you were eleven, did you believe the stork story?"

"No," Shawn muttered. "I am so sorry for letting the cat out of the bag, Preston. I had no idea it was a secret."

Jordan snorted. "And this would happen to only you."

Preston sighed. "Okay, we need to have this talk, you finished your breakfast. We can go upstairs and discuss it."

"Wait, before you go," Shawn said turning to her friend. "Everybody this is Carl Minto, my fiancé. He is only here for the day, so he won't be at your rehearsal, Saint. Don't worry he won't be crashing your party."

Shawn went around introducing them individually to her fiancé. Jordan still had his mouth opened.

Shawn went over to Jordan and then turned to Carl. "I was telling Carl that our wedding would have to be unconventional because I want you as my man of honor, Jordy."

Shawn looked up at a shell-shocked Jordan. "Isn't it perfect?"

Everybody was quiet for interminable seconds, Preston could hear the faucet drips into the sink and the blinds as the early morning breeze had them gently clanging against the wall.

It was as if time stood still. He was waiting for Jordan to explode.

Jordan cleared his throat instead. "Hey, Carl."

He shook Carl's hand and then stood back. "Man of honor huh? Sounds quite modern."

The brothers all breathed a collective sigh of relief. Even Carl seemed as if he breathed out too.

"Let's go, Pete," Preston said. "We have to talk."

He would leave them in the kitchen to work out the current tense situation. He had a little fire of his own to put out.

****

"I wanted to talk to you about this," Preston said sitting across from Pete in the living room. "I was thinking..."

"I love Aunty Sheryl," Pete said excitedly, "is she really

my mom?"

"Yes," Preston nodded, "she is."

"But how?" Pete was having a hard time processing it. "But..." was the only thing he said for a full minute.

Preston clasped his hands in front of his body. He had to connect the dots for his son as simply as he could.

"Her mother is Pamela Stone the lady you were looking for when you walked all the way from Westmoreland to Kingston. As I told you before, Miss Pam lived with us in Portland at that big house I showed you, Sheryl lived with us too."

"Uh huh," Pete nodded.

"We were very young when you were conceived, and Sheryl was not well at the time. Your grandmother Miss Pam, took her away to get her help and so we separated."

"And now she is back," Pete whispered, "but she hasn't said a word. Why hasn't she said anything to me?"

"Because she does not know that you are the son she gave away for adoption." Preston sighed. "She gave you up because she was very sick and couldn't care for you but she took one look at you when she initially saw you, and she was hooked."

"Are you going to tell her about me?" Pete asked.

"Oh yes." Preston nodded. "I will eventually. I have to. She loves you too much to deny her this. She never wants to talk about that time in her life, but I will force her to listen if I have to."

He got up and hugged Pete. "All of this will work out somehow. See, your prayer to God about finding your family is coming through more than you know."

"Aww," Walter said from the door. He had a lit candle in the middle of the muffin. "Shawn is grandstanding in the kitchen, and I need to do all the mushy birthday stuff before you leave for work."

"Because you know I hate it?" Preston said standing up from his hug with Pete.

"No," Walter snorted, "because I think you deserve a celebration of your life and I know you won't do it."

"Everybody come and sing happy birthday!" Walter yelled, "Preston looks like he is about to bolt."

They all sang him the happy birthday song, even Shawn's new guy who seemed surprisingly relaxed in their company.

"Make a wish," Walter said holding out the muffin, "and make it good."

Preston shook his head, "wishes are for kids."

"Unless you become like a little child, you will not enter the kingdom of God." Walter smiled. "Come on, do it."

Preston blew out the candle and closed his eyes in a childish gesture that made him feel ridiculous.

Please God let Sheryl and Pete, and I finally be the family that you want. He said it quietly and then he opened his eyes and looked at his brothers and Shawn sheepishly.

"I feel like an idiot. Thanks a lot."

****

He texted Sheryl on his way through the door after breakfast. *Are we still on for dinner at seven?*

The resulting yes came almost instantly, and then, "Happy birthday, hope you have a great day today."

He smiled all the way to the supermarket. When he reached his office, there were several bouquets of red roses on his desk.

"Helena?" He turned back to Helena's office. "Whose are these?"

"Yours." Helena grinned. "They arrived first thing this morning. I snooped and read one of the cards. It said roses are red violets are blue, may this day be joyful and filled with wonderful memories too. And it was signed SS."

Preston laughed. "I have never gotten flowers from a girl before."

"Well SS obviously thinks that it's time you did," Helena grinned. "By the way, happy birthday, boss. I gave my yearly contribution to the Alpha Boys Academy in lieu of your birthday gift as requested. Here is my receipt and your card."

"Thank you." Preston took the card and nodded. "You were generous this year."

"You are a generous employer, and I admire you for giving back. So I splurged this year."

Preston nodded. "That's great Helena, thank you."

"No, thank you for being the person you are," Helena said blinking her eyes rapidly. She cleared her throat. "I have something in my eyes. Anyway, I don't know of many persons being as generous and caring as you are and looking out for those less fortunate than yourself. It is amazing."

"I am just paying it forward," Preston said contemplatively, "fifteen years ago today when my mother decided to plunge the Wiley and Kennedy family into chaos I learned the power of community. Many persons have contributed to where my brothers and I are today. I like to never forget that."

Helena smiled. "SS is a lucky woman."

Chapter Twenty

"Sheryl Stone!" Noel growled before she could put down her handbag. "I would fire you now if Maci from head office did not beg me not to. You took two personal days, two!" Noel held up his fingers.

"Were you sick? No! Was it a death in the family? No!"

The veins at the side of Noel's head were practically bulging. "You decided that because your boyfriend's kid was sick, you could hightail it and go play mommy when we had an important meeting to attend. What do you have to say for yourself?"

"Nothing." Sheryl tried to talk quietly. She hoped that by lowering her voice, Noel would do the same.

"So you are having a crazy relapse then? Are you going to be mentally unstable again like you were as a teenager? It must be Jamaica or the air here that has you acting like a certifiable mental case!" Noel bellowed.

It hadn't worked. Sheryl was sure that the entire building was quiet and listening in. The office partitions were made from paper-thin walls. Now everybody would know she had a mental illness and that the boss wanted her gone.

"It has to be that you are going crazy again," Noel shouted. "I had Jamal Linton lined up for a meeting, I wanted my star sales person there, but you blew it off. I took Luna to the meeting instead, and Jamal Linton would not budge with his demands.

"Because of you, he is ordering even less of our products than before. I needed a star negotiator instead I got Luna who managed to irritate the man. I barely kept him from leaving all together. And yes, she is fired and you will be as well.

"You are of no use to this company if you are flitting off at your lover's bidding every chance you get!"

Sheryl inhaled. She had woken up feeling better this morning after spending most of her time cowering from her thoughts like an embarrassed lump yesterday. And now this. She could feel her head throbbing in response to the anger and sneer in Noel's face.

"I can fix it," She said calmly. "I can go to Jamal Linton office myself and talk to him."

Noel glared at her. "You are this close to pissing me off. This close. He held up his thumb and pointing finger to show a tiny space between them. And I don't care that you are bonded to this company. I am barely able to work with you now. Bonds can be broken or renegotiated. Do not for one minute think you are irreplaceable."

He flounced out of the office and slammed the door. The sound reverberated through the office.

Sheryl sighed. Noel had a right to be angry. She had acted pretty out of character when she had hightailed it to Pete's side when he was ill. She would probably be mad too if the shoe was on the other foot but Noel's jibes about her past mental illness was uncalled for.

It was private information that he was actually using against her on the job, and he had just made it public for the entire workforce to hear. She was sure they were out there whispering about it now.

What a way to out her. If she were mentally unstable, this would be enough cause a relapse. Besides that, it was unprofessional for him to blurt out her secret for everyone to hear.

She couldn't work with Noel a second more. The writing had been on the wall from the very start. He wanted to ruin her; it was there in his body language and in the blaze of hatred in his eyes.

He had been dying to share her secret with the office to discredit her. He was the last person she should have told about this. How could she have ever thought that she loved him enough to marry him?

Instead of picking up the phone to reset an appointment with Jamal Linton she picked up her giant calculator and tabulated how much money she would owe the company for her education. She then called head office and spoke to HR.

She hung up the phone after the conversation. She would have to pay back every single cent they had paid for college if she broke the terms of her employment bond contract now.

A good chunk of her house savings would be in peril, but she wouldn't be bonded to the company anymore. She would be free, and she would not have to deal with Noel.

She could go back home, find another job, forget all of this. She couldn't work at this place anymore. She didn't even know if she could hold her head up high when exiting the office but she had always been a fighter. This she could handle.

She called Maci first and then human resources. She had her resignation letter faxed by eleven. She was required to give a thirty-day notice but was told that she did not have to, obviously, Noel had called them first. She had no doubt he had painted her in the worst light possible.

She walked out of the office by twelve but then turned back. She loathed going back into the building. Everyone had looked at her earlier with the kind of awareness that they had heard what Noel had said and were assessing her as she left. She needed to tell Noel to his face that he had gotten his greatest wish.

She gritted her teeth and went through the front door. She still had some time left with Carragon. She had to vacate the apartment by the end of the month, which was four days, and then return the company car by tomorrow.

At least there was one bright spot left for the day; she still had dinner with Preston to celebrate his birthday. She wouldn't breathe a word about this to him.

She knocked on Noel's door and heard his gruff, "Come in."

Sheryl stood at the door, not trusting herself to go any further. "You got your wish. I am out of here."

Noel glared at her. "Good riddance to bad rubbish."

Sheryl gasped. "Okay then."

She closed back the door and headed out of Carragon offices for good.

****

Preston didn't know why he was nervous. Maybe it was the fact that since he had picked up Sheryl at six-thirty, she was looking a little off. Not physically. Physically she was gorgeous as usual dressed in a green halter neck dress with ruffles at the neck. It emphasized her toned arms and her svelte shape. Her hair was out in all of its long think glory. She looked like an exotic queen. He had a hard time looking away from her.

But behind her eyes looked sad. Tired. Defeated. He had a sense that tonight was not the right night to be having any heavy conversations. He was determined to keep it light.

"What's wrong?" He asked almost as soon as she got in the car.

"Nothing is wrong." Sheryl smiled at him. "I had a tough day that's all. I don't want to talk about it on your birthday."

Preston frowned. "I can handle it. My birthdays tend to be the days for unsavory things. Trust me; I can deal with whatever it is that's bugging you."

"No." Sheryl smiled at him, "Tonight is about Saint and Sandrene and you. It's a celebration."

"Oh no, it's not about any of us, you stole my thunder." Preston winked at her. "I can't concentrate on anything else but you. You look simply beautiful."

Sheryl smiled. "Thank you. I have to pull out all the stops when I am with the handsome Preston Wiley. Who is always on top of his style game."

Preston grinned. "You know I try."

"You don't have to try," Sheryl smirked. "You never did. You were just born with it."

Preston laughed. "You could sound happier about it."

"Nope." Sheryl shook her head. "Poor Pete looks like you, pretty soon girls will be all over him. Poor baby. Where is he though? I thought he was attending."

"Yes he is, but he is a part of the band." Preston shrugged. "He will be doing a duet with Case. They left together."

"So he is completely better then." Sheryl sighed. "I called him today. I needed to hear his voice for myself. He sounded thrilled to hear from me."

"Yes." Preston looked at her, "he loves you."

"It's mutual." Sheryl looked through the window and didn't say anything else for a very long time.

Preston turned on his CD player to fill in the loaded silence. He wondered what Sheryl was thinking. The smooth sounds of Lauryn Hill came on, Can't Take My Eyes Off You.

He was nodding his head to the music, and Sheryl turned to him and started singing. He grinned. Her voice sounded like a good approximation of Lauryn Hill's.

She sang all the way to the restaurant even having him join in with her. It was fun. When they reached the venue, they were still laughing.

Her somber mood had lifted, and she didn't look as sad behind the eyes. There was genuine mirth and happiness on her face now.

Preston wondered what had caused the sadness in the first place. He hated to see her upset.

"Sheryl!" Shawn squealed when they reached the reception area. She seemed as if she was having a tense conversation with Jordan.

Jordan looked relieved when Shawn turned from him and headed for Sheryl. They hugged like long lost friends.

Preston went over to his brother. "How is it going man-of-honor?"

"She is doing this to wind me up. Her boyfriend has to be the most accepting, accommodating creature on the planet to be accommodating a male friend in his so-called fiancé's life," Jordan growled. "I am playing along for now. Stop calling me man-of-honor."

Preston chuckled. A passing waiter brought them drinks.

Sandrene and Saint came over, and they spoke a while. The live band started playing, Beres Hammond, *I Am In*

Love With You.

The place was decorated in white, gray and silver. The atmosphere was convivial. Sheryl and Shawn were talking and laughing with each other.

A constant flow of friends and acquaintances came over to make small talk.

Sheryl went over and whispered to Preston that she was going to the restroom. He was in the middle of a conversation with Sandrene's father, Lamar Russell.

"There are at least a hundred people here," Lamar said proudly, "quite a crowd for a rehearsal dinner, isn't Gracie, a good planner?"

"Well, it's tastefully done," Preston said to the proud father of the bride.

"You both are single aren't you?" Lamar asked casually. "My Gracie is single too you know?"

Preston and Jordan looked at each other in horror.

"And here she is!" Lamar waved when Gracie entered the reception hall in a plunging front red dress. She had her hands entwined with a man who was looking around the venue.

"She seems taken already, Lamar," Jordan said in relief.

Preston was trying to place the guy that Gracie was with. He looked familiar. Tall, urbane, gray eyes.

"Hello everyone." Gracie beamed at them and gave her father an affectionate peck. "Let me introduce my date for the night, Noel Paul."

"From Carragon Jamaica Ltd," Noel added. "I met Gracie a few days ago, and we hit it off."

"A businessman." Lamar beamed. "I am her father, Lamar Russell."

"And this is Preston Wiley." Gracie licked her lips when she looked at him, "and Jordan Wiley, brothers to the groom."

"Oh, I recognized Preston," Noel said politely. "We do

business together."

"That's right." Preston nodded. That's where he knew the guy from; he was Sheryl's current boss, her ex-fiancé.

Preston and Jordan shook his hand, but they didn't get into any small talk. They got distracted with another friend who exuberantly greeted them.

Preston would have given no thought about Noel Paul for the rest of the night except that when Sheryl and Shawn came into his line of vision, he saw the change in Noel's facial expression. He twisted his face, and there was a sneer in his eyes when he saw Sheryl.

Something was obviously not right there. Even more noteworthy was the way that Sheryl, who had been animatedly talking to Shawn, stopped midstep and looked scared as if she had seen a ghost when she saw Noel.

Chapter Twenty-One

Sheryl could not believe her eyes. Was Noel stalking her? What were the odds that they would end up at the same party a few hours after he had basically called her trash? Very low odds.

She made a beeline for their table. Hoping feverishly that Noel was placed far, very far away from where she was to sit. If she could get through tonight with Noel and his hateful presence, she would be fine.

They were at table six, almost in the middle of the room. The table could seat eight she was going to be among friends. She read the rest of the cute little place settings with Saint and Sandrene's picture on it. She was to sit between Preston and Jordan. Shawn was to the right of them and then she saw Guy plus-one and Walter plus-one. She didn't know who their plus-ones were, but she knew it wouldn't be Noel.

Sheryl made a sigh of relief and then sat down.

"You okay?" Preston sat beside her. "You saw your boss

and looked spooked for a while."

"Do you think he saw me?" Sheryl whispered.

"Yes he did, and he had a strange expression on his face. I wanted to ask him about that, but I didn't get a chance to, too many friends wanting to say hello.

"What's going on?" Preston frowned, "you two had a fight or something?"

"I promised I wouldn't say a thing until this evening is through," Sheryl murmured near his ear, "and I am keeping my promise."

"Okay." Preston looked at her with concern.

"Oh, hey everybody." A breathy voiced girl came over to their table in a red dress that looked like a sneeze would expose her feminine assets.

"Walter and Guy do not have a plus-one, so there is a reshuffle," she continued. "My date and I will sit here. Gives me easy access to the rest of the room. Everybody, this is Noel. Make him feel at home please."

Sheryl's heart sank when she saw that it was the Noel. No doubt about it he had seen her. He sat across from her and Preston and looked at them with narrowed eyes.

"Uh-oh," Preston whistled under his breath. "I sense trouble."

"My night is officially ruined," Sheryl whispered back.

"Maybe I should introduce myself to the table since we are going to spend the night together," Noel said a hard glint in his gaze as he looked at her.

"I already know Sheryl she worked for me."

"As in past tense?" Preston asked looking between both Sheryl and Noel.

"That's right." Noel leaned forward. "Sheryl is no longer at Carragon Ltd. She left today."

"Is that so?" Preston shook the hand offered to him.

Curiosity was obviously eating him alive.

Noel shook hands with Jordan, Shawn, Guy, and Walter and then relaxed in his chair. "It's lovely to meet business partners and at a social function too," Noel said to the Wiley's.

Sheryl was holding herself like a wound up string. She didn't trust Noel's seemingly relaxed sprawl nor did she trust the way he kept on looking between her and Preston his eyes narrowed and assessing.

She was partially relieved when everybody was seated, and the MC started her energetic games. The first icebreaker game was getting to know those at your table.

Papers and pens were handed out.

They were supposed to put their table numbers and then write memories or assumptions about persons at the table and then the rest of the table would guess who it is they were talking about.

Table one's assumptions were hilarious. One of Sandrene's aunts had dyed her hair green by accident and had to go to an interview with it because she couldn't reverse it in time. Another of the guests had swum with sharks.

By the time they had reached her table, Sheryl had gotten into the spirit of things and was having fun despite Noel sitting across from her.

The MC read out loud, "Table six, whose birthday is it today and what is his favorite gift."

"That's easy." Shawn raised her hand and spoke into the mike. "It's Preston's birthday today, and his favorite charity is the Alpha boys home, and that is where he likes us to send his gifts."

"Well then, let's sing happy birthday to one of the groom's brothers. Bring out the cake we have for him."

"I can't believe you guys did this." Preston glared at his

brothers, as the cake came out and everybody belted out the birthday song.

"Happy birthday, Preston," Sheryl whispered after the song.

Preston curled his fingers around hers and squeezed. "It feels like a happy birthday, finally."

The MC continued with the game and picked up another paper from her bowl. "Which girl sitting at table six was enrolled as a boy in high school for a full year."

"Shawn!" Everybody yelled the answer.

The MC chuckled, "I need to hear that story."

She picked up another paper.

"Who sitting at table six had a mental problem, was promiscuous when she was younger and gave up her baby for…"

There was dead silence.

The MC looked embarrassed and was trying hard to recover. "Er, this was obviously a mistake."

But nobody was listening to her anymore. All eyes were on table six.

Sheryl stiffened. She couldn't move if someone forced her to.

Noel raised a hand and casually said to the silent room. "I know the answer to that, my former employee, Sheryl Stone. I am betting that her current date Preston Wiley would be grateful for this information."

"No he wouldn't," Preston growled. "What's wrong with you, Noel!"

Noel looked at him with a calculating glint in his eye. "I am not joking. You should take heed. Sheryl is pretty to look at, but all that glitters is not gold. She had mental problems, and she was a slut."

Sheryl still could not move she hung her head like

somebody was forcing her to look down at the table.

When she left Jamaica, she would never come back. Never. One hundred and odd people, some of them strangers, knew her secret.

The MC had speedily moved on to table seven. Table six was oddly silent.

"We know about Sheryl, you moron," Shawn hissed at Noel. "We were there when Sheryl met in that tragic accident that messed her up mentally. You are sitting at a table with people who know her from she was a little girl. What kind of a monster are you to even write that on a piece of paper and then sit back looking smug?"

"He is the kind of monster that we don't do business with," Walter added. "Prepare to be dropped by Wiley Incorporated, Noel. We will be dropping every lipstick, every shampoo, every bar of soap your company carries! We are loyal to our friends and Sheryl is our friend."

Noel's eyes swung from one disapproving face to the other. "Oh, but I thought..."

"You thought that you could humiliate Sheryl and then have us all running for our lives after we heard her secrets?" Preston growled. "Nobody hurts the woman that I love and gets away with it scot-free. You just made an enemy."

"Seven enemies." Shawn hissed. "That was a low down thing to do, moron."

"And while we are on the subject of secrets." Preston inhaled raggedly. "Sheryl look at me."

"Sheryl," Preston whispered in her ear.

"What?" Sheryl's voice was choked up she could barely get the 'what' to squeeze out.

"That baby you gave up for adoption is Pete. He is our son. Yours and mine. I want you to stop being ashamed of the adoption, and I want us to discuss this frankly, okay."

Sheryl looked at Preston tears at the corner of her eyes. "What? How? Isn't Jaylee his mother?"

"No." Preston cupped her chin in his hand. "You are."

He turned fiery eyes to Noel, "Get out! This is a Wiley event. This is the first of a very costly mistake you just made."

Chapter Twenty-Two

Sheryl hardly registered the rest of the engagement party, but she remembered getting quite a few sympathizing pats and nods when she had exited the venue with Preston in tow. Pete had been getting ready with Case and had completely missed the drama from earlier that evening.

"Explain." Sheryl had stopped in the middle of the parking lot before they even reached the car. "Tell me how Pete is mine."

"Your heart already knew," Preston said. "I was patiently waiting for you to bring up, the adoption or at least connect the dots. I did you a disservice twelve years ago, and I want to tell you I am sorry."

Sheryl closed her eyes and then opened them. "Pete is my son?"

"Yes, he is." Preston nodded. "Come on let's have this long overdue conversation in the car."

Sheryl nodded. "Please."

She sat down in the passenger seat and then looked at Preston in mortification. "One hundred and eight persons now know about my past."

"It doesn't matter what one hundred persons think," Preston said. "I think you are great and I love you, and I want us to be a family."

"I can't," Sheryl whispered in horror. "I can't show my face in this country again. I have four days to leave my apartment, and then I am booking my flight home."

Preston sighed. "I met Pete three months ago; he walked from Westmoreland to Kingston to search for his grandmother, he prayed for a chance to meet his real family."

Sheryl didn't think she closed her mouth while Preston laid out exactly what happened up to the point when she called him at his office to sell him products.

"I was shocked when the very woman who I was looking for was the one who was on the line and sounding defensive about her past."

"Oh goodness," Sheryl murmured.

"So, I am asking you not for my sake alone but for Pete's sake. Stay here with us. We love you."

"He knows?" Sheryl cleared her throat, "that I am his mother?"

"Oh yes, and the boy is as happy as can be about it."

Sheryl laughed and then closed her eyes. "Pinch me, Preston, because I know this is a dream and I am about to wake up. Of course, I will stay, I love you so much, and I love Pete.

"I might never leave the house though, because I am embarrassed and probably will not be going out much after this, but I would never leave you now."

"I won't pinch you," Preston gathered her in his arms," but I will do this."

The kiss was a promise, new and yet familiar.

"I asked Pastor Tate," Preston whispered against her lips. "You remember him?"

"Of course, I remember him," Sheryl said distractedly. She could barely concentrate when he was so near.

"We can get married on the beach at my cottage in two days." Preston picked up her hand and intertwined it with his. "I don't want to upstage my brother, but I think we should get married soon. No engagement parties or rehearsal dinners and all of that jazz. I just want us to be together, the sooner, the better."

"I agree." Sheryl chuckled. "Oh Preston, I am so happy. Terrified and happy."

"No need to be terrified, only happy." Preston deepened the kiss.

****

Three days later in the morning, the Wiley brothers, Shawn, Pete and a handful of their Portland friends were standing on the beach witnessing the nuptials of Preston Wiley and Sheryl Stone.

They had waited an extra day for Miss Pam to book a flight. She had arrived late last night but had been up with the birds a pleased smile on her face. She had her hands clasped in Pete's.

"This is the right time and the right place, for this to happen," she looked down in her grandson's precious face.

"And now these three remain: faith, hope, and love," Pastor Tate said in his blessing, "but the greatest of these is love."

"You may kiss your bride, Preston Wiley."

Preston did just that.

The End

Author's Notes

Dear Reader,

I really hoped you liked For Pete's Sake another installment in the Wiley Brother's series. I enjoyed writing, Preston and Sheryl's story. Yes, you will see them again in other books, the Wiley Series will span a number of years.

Coming up next is **Crossing Jordan**. An excerpt is a page flip away.

Thanks again. All the best,

Brenda

"Don't you just love weddings?" Shawn asked in the silence. She had opted to drive down with Jordan from Preston's villa after the reception.

Jordan wished she had driven her own car. He was not in the mood for company, especially her company.

"Weddings are okay," Jordan answered flippantly. He was happy for Preston and Sheryl, but he was in a strange mood.

He felt restless, uneasy, just a little bit melancholy. He felt as if he was being left behind, though he didn't want to examine that last bit of errant emotion closely. His lack of sleep was contributing to his dark mood, he was sure. All he needed was some good uninterrupted sleep, and then he would be back on an even keel.

"You sound grumpy." Shawn looked at him and grinned. "I wonder why? Are you feeling jealous that Preston has found happiness and you are still out in the cold? You are still single and unloved?"

Jordan looked at Shawn and chuckled. "Single yes, unloved, no. You love me. You love me enough to ask me to be the man-of-honor at your wedding. I am honored, truly I am. This is the height of true love for one friend to another."

Shawn stopped grinning and scowled at Jordan. "Why do I doubt the sincerity of that statement?"

"Because you are paranoid?" Jordan glanced at Shawn. "By the way, where is your hulky fiancé, Carl? I thought you would have taken him as a date to the wedding?"

"He has a magazine shoot to do today," Shawn mumbled. "It was booked months in advance. That is why he is in Jamaica."

"I see." Jordan smiled at her. "He is a model?"

"Not a model. He owns a fitness club he is promoting his franchises out here, and as you can see, his body is a testament to how fit a man can get." Shawn's voice was surly, "Why are you so interested in him?"

"Because we are best friends and he is your fiancé." Jordan slowed down the car to allow several goats to cross the road. "Wouldn't you be curious too when I bring the woman who I want to marry for you to meet?"

Shawn inhaled raggedly and bit her lip. "You don't have a woman in your life."

"I should address that," Jordan said contemplatively. "I have been single far too long."

"You don't tell me about your girlfriends." Shawn looked at him accusingly, "you never share that side of your life with me."

"Unlike you," Jordan snorted, "who will overshare every little thing that's happening in your love life in nauseating detail. That begs the question, why have I not heard of Carl before?"

Shawn frowned at him, "I told you about him. I called you when you were in Dubai. I told you I met him two months ago at a health food store."

"I must have been half asleep," Jordan murmured.

"You were," Shawn smirked. "I told you I was living healthier this year and that I met this bodybuilder guy who I think might be the one."

"Oh yes, one of your health based conversations." Jordan raked his eyes over her body; she looked very healthy to him—fit as usual because of her job and her hiking and other hobbies. Shawn could not sit still to save her life.

She was in a simple lavender shift dress. Her hair was in a stylish curly chignon with little white flowers around the loose knot at her neck. It looked like one of Jackie's styles. Shawn did not wear her hair like this without Jackie's intervention.

She looked pretty and sophisticated; he had to admit grudgingly. He hated that he still noticed and still thought of her like this.

He had been running away from his feelings for Shawn for years. It had driven him all the way to Dubai. Maybe it was time for him to stop running and to face his feelings. He didn't want to lose her to Carl, the bodybuilder.

"Are you listening to me?" Shawn clipped her fingers.

"Yes," Jordan nodded, "you met Carl and thought he was the one."

He drove up to the house and parked. "Do you want me to drop you over at Jackie's place or are you coming inside?"

"I am coming inside." Shawn got out of the car and slammed the door before Jordan could react.

He opened the front door and stepped aside so that she could precede him.

She flounced into the house and then stood in the middle of the living room her hands akimbo, foot tapping. "Why are you so calm about this?"

"About what?" Jordan asked tiredly. He sank down in one of the settees and closed his eyes.

"About me getting married to Carl? Five years ago you went berserk when I introduced you to Paul."

Jordan cracked an eye open and then closed it again. "You didn't introduce me to Paul. I caught Paul in your apartment in the early hours of the morning, half naked. Five years ago I thought that I would break out of my friend box with you and finally we could be together and then I learned that you didn't view us the same way I did."

"It wasn't what you thought with Paul." Shawn

interjected, "I keep on telling you the same thing. It was a misunderstanding. He was at my apartment sleeping on the sofa. You overreacted to a perfectly innocent situation."

Jordan frowned. "Shawn give it up. I don't need explanations. We are cool now, aren't we? Five years ago I was jealous. I was under the misguided impression that you and I were going somewhere. Five years ago I cared."

"But you don't care now?" Shawn almost whispered the question.

"I wouldn't say I don't care but..." Jordan mumbled sleepily, kicked off his shoes and curled up on the sofa. "None of this matters anyway. I am going to renew my contract with Blue Corals. There is so much work to do in Dubai."

"But why?" Shawn asked plaintively.

"Why work?" Jordan asked lazily, looking up at Shawn as she paced from one end of the living room to the other.

"No, why leave. I was planning to come back home, and we could hang out again like old times, we could..."

"No thanks," Jordan visibly shuddered, "I can't see myself hanging out with you and Carl. I hate being the third wheel."

Shawn sat across from Jordan and sighed in exasperation, "Jordy, please don't leave again."

"Why should I stay?" Jordan sat up and leaned on his elbows. "There is no incentive for me to stay. My brothers are getting married one by one. Preston is married. You are going to get married. I have no..."

He didn't get the chance to finish the statement. Shawn pulled her dress over her head and stood in her black lace underwear.

"Is this incentive enough?"

Jordan widened his eyes and then coughed. "Shawn do not play with me. Why do you do stuff like this?"

"I am not playing," Shawn said determinedly. "You want

incentive I'll give you incentive. Isn't this what both of us have been tiptoeing around for years?"

"Put your clothes back on," Jordan said a glint in his eyes. "You are getting married to Carl, aren't you? I wouldn't be a good man-of-honor if I took advantage of the bride."

OTHER BOOKS BY BRENDA BARRETT

Wiley Brothers Series

Between Brothers (Book 0)- The beginning of the Wiley brothers saga, Joseph Wiley's unconventional family life may prove to be fatal to some members of the family.

For Pete's Sake (Book 1)- Preston has a run in with a child named Pete who claims that he is the grandson of their former housekeeper Pamela Stone.

Crossing Jordan (Book 2)- Jordan is miffed when Shawn takes her new fiancé to Jamaica and insists that he be best man at their wedding.

Fire and Walter (Book 3)- Walter's shady past is affecting his new appointment as church elder. The situation would not only compromise him but a particular newly married church sister as well.

The Perfect Guy (Book 4) - Guy decides to explore the world of farming, becomes an apprentice to a farmer and lives a humble life. He is constantly rebuffed by the woman that he loves because she thinks he is poor!

The Patience of A Saint (Book 5)- Saint attends his own divorce party put on by his soon to be ex wife and they end up complicating matters.

A Case of Love (Book 6)- Case unwittingly buys a bride from a human trafficking ring a few days before his own wedding.

Resetter Series

Never Too Late (Book 1)- Addi finds out she is a resetter and goes back to the summer of 92 to change her family's lives.

Never Say Never (Book 2)- Skyler's handsome college lecturer, who happens to be her neighbor, has a 't' in his palms. Should she tell him the significance of it. If she does, would he believe her?

Now or Never (Book 3)- Ten years later Addi and Randy meet again at Randy's engagement party. Why is it that the chemistry between them was still so potent? Can they ever have a future together? Would Randy choose her this time around?

Almost Never (Book 4)- Tech genius Joshua Porter had all but given up on love. He then meets Portia, an inmate at the female penitentiary and his life takes a turn for the adventurous.

The Scarlett Family Series

Scarlett Baby (Book 1)- When the head of the Scarlett family died, Yuri had to return home to Treasure Beach for the funeral. What he didn't count on was seeing Marla, his childhood sweetheart and his best friend's wife. And when emotions overwhelm them and a few months later Marla is pregnant, Yuri wants the impossible: his best friend's wife and the baby they made together...

Scarlett Sinner (Book 2)- Pastor Troy Scarlett realizes the hard way that some sins are bound to be revealed, like the child that he had out of wedlock with his wife's mortal enemy from college. His wife Chelsea was not happy with the status quo. She was not taking care of the son of the woman she had so despised from college. And she could not get over the deep betrayal that she felt from her husband's indiscretion.

Scarlett Secret (Book 3)- Terri Scarlett had a soft spot for her friend, Lola. She was funny and sweet and they looked remarkably alike. But when Lola's Arab prince demands his bride, Terri foolishly exchange places with her friend and they meet up on a world of trouble.

Scarlett Love (Book 4)- Slater always looked forward to delivering packages to the law firm where he could get a glimpse of the stunning female lawyer, Amoy Gardener. Unfortunately, for Slater a woman like Amoy would not take him seriously, especially when she found out that he could not read!

Scarlett Promise (Book 5)- Driven by desperation Lisa Barclay decides to make some extra money by prostituting herself after being kicked out in the streets. Her first customer turns out to be a popular government senator and then to her horror he dies...

Scarlett Bride (Book 6)- When Oliver Scarlett's missionary work in the Congo region was coming to an end, he had a decision to make, marry Ashaki Azanga and save her from being the fourth wife to the chief of the village or leave her to her fate and get on with his life...

Scarlett Heart (Book 7)- After receiving a heart transplant shy librarian Noah Scarlett started to take on character traits that were unlike him and he kept dreaming of a girl named Cassandra Green...

Rebound Series

On The Rebound- For Better or Worse, Brandon vowed to stay with Ashley, but when worse got too much he moved out and met Nadine. For the first time in years he felt happy, but then Ashley remembered her wedding vows...

On The Rebound 2- Ashley reinvented herself and was now a first lady in a country church in Primrose Hill, but her obsessed ex friend Regina showed up and started digging into the lives of the saints at church. Somebody didn't like Regina's digging. Someone had secrets that were shocking enough to kill for...

Magnolia Sisters

Dear Mystery Guy (Book 1)- Della Gold details her life in a journal dedicated to a mystery guy. But when fascination turns into obsession she finds herself wanting to learn even more about him but in her pursuit of the mystery guy she begins to learn more about herself...

Bad Girl Blues (Book 2)- Brigid Manderson wanted to go to med school but for the time being she was an escort working for her mother, an ex-prostitute. When her latest customer offers her the opportunity of a lifetime would she take it? Or would she choose the harder path and uncertain love with a Christian guy?

Her Mistaken Dreams (Book 3)- Caitlin Denvers dream guy had serious issues. He has a dead wife in his past and he was the main suspect in her murder. Did he really do it? Or did Caitlin for the first time have a mistaken dream?

Just Like Yesterday (Book 4)- Hazel Brown lost six months of memory including the summer that she conceived her son, and had no idea who his father could be. Now that she had the means to fight to get him back from the Deckers, she finds out that the handsome Curtis Decker is willing to share her son with her after all.

New Song Series

Going Solo (Book 1)- Carson Bell, had a lovely voice, a heart of gold, and was no slouch in the looks department. So why did Alice abandon him and their daughter? What did she want after ten years of silence?

Duet on Fire (Book 2)- Ian and Ruby had problems trying to conceive a child. If that wasn't enough, her ex-lover the current pastor of their church wants her back...

Tangled Chords (Book 3)- Xavier Bell, the poor, ugly duckling has made it rich and his looks have been incredibly improved too. Farrah Knight, hotel heiress had cruelly rejected him in the past but now she needed help. Could Xavier forgive and forget?

Broken Harmony(Book 4)- Aaron Lee, wanted the top job in his family company but he had a moral clause to consider just when Alka, his married ex-girlfriend walks back into his life.

A Past Refrain (Book 5)- Jayce had issues with forgetting Haley Greenwald even though he had a new woman in his life. Will he ever be able to shake his love for Haley?

Perfect Melody (Book 6)- Logan Moore had the perfect wife, Melody but his secretary Sabrina was hell bent on breaking up the family. Sabrina wanted Logan whatever the cost and she had a secret about Melody, that could shatter Melody's image to everyone.

The Bancroft Family Series

Homely Girl (Book 0) - April and Taj were opposites in so many ways. He was the cute, athletic boy that everybody wanted to be friends with. She was the overweight, shy, and withdrawn girl. Do April and Taj have a love that can last a lifetime? Or will time and separate paths rip them apart?

Saving Face (Book 1) - Mount Faith University drama begins with a dead president and several suspects including the president in waiting Ryan Bancroft.

Tattered Tiara (Book 2) - Micah Bancroft is targeted by femme fatale Deidra Durkheim. There are also several rape cases to be solved.

Private Dancer (Book 3) Adrian Bancroft was gutted when he returned to Jamaica and found out that his first and only love Cathy Taylor was a stripper and was literally owned by the menacing drug lord, Nanjo Jones.

Goodbye Lonely (Book 4) - Kylie Bancroft was shy and had to resort to going to confidence classes. How could she win the love of Gareth Beecher, her faculty adviser, a man with a jealous ex-wife in his past and a current mystery surrounding a hand found in his garden?

Practice Run (Book 5) - Marcus Bancroft had many reasons to avoid Mount Faith but Deidra Durkheim was not one of them. Unfortunately, on one of his visits he was the victim of a deliberate hit and run.

Sense of Rumor (Book 6) - Arnella Bancroft was the wild, passionate Bancroft, the creative loner who didn't mind living dangerously; but when a terrible thing happened to her at her friend Tracy's party, it changed her. She found that courting rumors can be devastating and that only the truth could set her free.

A Younger Man (Book 7)- Pastor Vanley Bancroft loved Anita Parkinson despite their fifteen-year age gap, but Anita had a secret, one that she could not reveal to Vanley. To tell him would change his feelings toward her, or force him to give up the ministry that he loved so much.

Just To See Her (Book 8)- Jessica Bancroft had the opportunity to meet her fantasy guy Khaled, he was finally coming to Mount Faith but she had feelings for Clay Reid, a guy who had all the qualities she was looking for. Who would she choose and what about the weird fascination Khaled had for Clay?

The Three Rivers Series

Private Sins (Book 1)- Kelly, the first lady at Three Rivers Church was pregnant for the first elder of her church. Could she keep the secret from her husband and pretend that all was well?

Loving Mr. Wright (Book 2)- Erica saw one last opportunity to ditch her single life when Caleb Wright appeared in her town. He was perfect for her, but what was he hiding?

Unholy Matrimony (Book 3) - Phoebe had a problem, she was poor and unhappy. Her solution to marry a rich man was derailed along the way with her feelings for Charles Black, the poor guy next door.

If It Ain't Broke (Book 4)- Chris Donahue wanted a place in his child's life. Pinky Black just wanted his love. She also wanted him to forget his obsession with Kelly and love her. That shouldn't be so hard? Should it?

Contemporary Romance/Drama

After The End--Torn between two lovers. Colleen married her high school sweetheart, Isaiah, hoping that they would live happily ever after but life intruded and Isaiah disappeared at sea. She found work with the rich and handsome, Enrique Lopez, as a housekeeper and realized that she couldn't keep him at arms length...

Love Triangle: Three Sides To The Story- George, the husband, Marie, the wife and Karen-the mistress. They all get to tell their side of the story.

The Preacher And The Prostitute - Prostitution and the clergy don't mix. Tell that to ex-prostitute, Maribel, who finds herself in love with the Pastor at her church. Can an ex-prostitute and a pastor have a future together?

New Beginnings - Inner city girl Geneva was offered an opportunity of a lifetime when she found out that her 'real' father was a very wealthy man. Her decision to live up-town meant that she had to leave Froggie, her 'ghetto don,' behind. She also found herself battling with her stepmother and battling her emotions for Justin, a suave up-towner.

Full Circle - After graduating from university, Diana wanted to return to Jamaica to find her siblings. What she didn't foresee was that she would meet Robert Cassidy and that both their pasts would be intertwined, and that disturbing questions would pop up about their parentage, just when they were getting close.

Historical Fiction/Romance

The Empty Hammock - Workaholic, Ana Mendez, fell asleep in a hammock and woke up in the year 1494. It was the time of the Tainos, a time when life seemed simpler, but Ana knew that all of that was about to change.

The Pull Of Freedom - Even in bondage the people, freshly arrived from Africa, considered themselves free. Led by Nanny and Cudjoe the slaves escaped the Simmonds' plantation and went in different directions to forge their destiny in the new country called Jamaica.

Jamaican Comedy (Material contains Jamaican dialect)

Di Taxi Ride And Other Stories- Di Taxi Ride and Other Stories is a collection of twelve witty and fast paced short stories. Each story tells of a unique slice of Jamaican life.

NOTA DEL AUTOR

En el presente relato intenté no mezclar lo antiguo con lo moderno. Evitar los disparates, los anacronismos, los adornos superfluos, comparar diversos párrafos del *Vetusta scribent nescio quo pacto antiquus fit animus*, no mezclar jamás nuestros conceptos modernos a las antiguas formas de pensar y sentir, tal fue mi deseo, mi esfuerzo, y, sin duda, mi quimera. Pero mi texto está bastante compuesto; y si yo quisiera indicar en detalle sus fuentes, necesitaría poner al pie de las páginas de este pequeño libro tantas notas como las que puso Bec de Fouquières a los poemas de André Chénier. En todo caso, me siento obligado a dar a los lectores las siguientes indicaciones generales:

Los fragmentos que se conservan de los antiguos poemas franceses han sido, en su mayor parte, publicados por Francisque Michel: *Tristan, recueil de ce qui reste des poèmes relatif à ses aventures.* (París, Techener, 1835-1839).

El Capítulo I de nuestra novela (Las mocedades) lo compuse basándome en diversos poemas, sobre todo, en el poema de Thomas. –Los Capítulos II (El Morholt) y III (La Bella) los compuse basándome en Eilhart d'Oberg (Edition Lichtenstein, Strasbourg, 1878). –Para escribir el Capítulo IV (El Filtro), me inspiré en el conjunto de la tradición, sobre todo, en el relato de Eilhart. Algunos trozos los tomé de Gottfried de Strasbourg (édit. W.

Goltherm, Berlin et Stuttgart, 1888). –Capítulo V (Brangien): tomado de Eilhart. –Capítulo VI (El alto pino). En la mitad de este capítulo, cuando Isolda acude a la cita junto al pino, empieza el fragmento de Béroul, que seguí fielmente en los Capítulos VII (El enano Frocino), VIII (El salto), IX (El bosque), X (Fray Ogrino) y XI (El vado), modificando aquí y allá el relato para recurrir al poema de Eilhart. –Capítulo XII (La ordalía): Resumen bastante libre del fragmento anónimo que sigue al fragmento de Béroul. –Capítulo XIII (La voz del ruiseñor): Intercalado siguiendo un poema didáctico del siglo XIII: el Domnel Amanz. –Capítulo XIV (El cascabel): Sacado de Gottfried de Strasbourg. –Capítulos XV (Isolda las de las Blancas Manos), XVI (Kaherdin) y XVII (Dinas de Lidan): Los episodios de Kariado y de Tristán leproso están sacados de Thomas; el resto está tratado, en general, siguiendo a Eilhart. –Capítulo XVIII (La locura): Adaptación de un corto poema francés, episódico e independiente. –Capítulo XIX (La muerte): Traducido de Thomas. Algunos episodios están tomados de Eilhart y de la novela en prosa francesa contenida en los manuscritos 103 del Fondo Francés de la Bibliotèque National, París.

Joseph Bédier